The Jumbies

"A scary but cheerful tale that draws on Caribbean folk traditions. A great update on the 'town under supernatural attack' story, with a marvelous setting." —*The Baltimore Sun*

"Endlessly addictive and hypnotic." —*Essence*

Rise of the Jumbies

★ "A stellar recommendation for fans of edgy fantasy such as Aaron Starmer's Riverman Trilogy or Adam Gidwitz's A Tale Dark and Grimm series, and, of course, fans of the first book." —*School Library Journal*, starred review

★ "A stirring and mystical tale sure to keep readers thinking past the final page." —*Kirkus Reviews*, starred review

"If you're looking for a story that's original, action packed and inspiring, look no further than *Rise of the Jumbies*." —*BookPage*

The Jumbie God's Revenge

★ "Baptiste engages all the senses, from the taste of sweet oranges to the scent of salty air . . . [Corinne's] determination, compassion, and bravery will inspire readers to face down any challenges crossing their paths . . . A tremendous return." —*Kirkus Reviews*, starred review

"Highly recommend for middle-grade readers who enjoy brave heroines, facing the odds, and magic." —YA Books Central

"Packed with action . . . Readers will be as enthralled by the heartening tenacity and perseverance of friendship and community as by the jumbies and humans confronting a dangerous deity." —*The Horn Book Magazine*

Praise for the Jumbies Series

The
JUMBIE
GOD'S
REVENGE

THE JUMBIES SERIES BY TRACEY BAPTISTE

The Jumbies

Rise of the Jumbies

The Jumbie God's Revenge

The JUMBIE GOD'S REVENGE

Tracey Baptiste

ALGONQUIN YOUNG READERS 2021

Published by
Algonquin Young Readers
an imprint of Algonquin Books of Chapel Hill
Post Office Box 2225
Chapel Hill, North Carolina 27515-2225

a division of
Workman Publishing
225 Varick Street
New York, New York 10014

First paperback edition, Algonquin Young Readers, March 2021.
Originally published in hardcover by Algonquin Young Readers in September 2019.

Printed in the United States of America.
Published simultaneously in Canada by Thomas Allen & Son Limited.
Design by Carla Weise.

LIBRARY OF CONGRESS CATALOGING-IN-PUBLICATION DATA
Names: Baptiste, Tracey, author.
Title: The jumbie god's revenge / Tracey Baptiste.
Description: First edition. | Chapel Hill, North Carolina : Algonquin Young
Readers, 2019. | Summary: After two out-of-season hurricanes nearly
destroy her island home, Corinne discovers that the god Huracan is angry
and she, aided by friends and enemies alike, races to calm him.
Identifiers: LCCN 2019006071 | ISBN 9781616208912 (hardcover : alk. paper)
Subjects: | CYAC: Hurricanes—Fiction. | Gods—Fiction. | Spirits—Fiction. |
Magic—Fiction. | Islands—Fiction. | Blacks—Caribbean Area—Fiction. |
Caribbean Area—Fiction.
Classification: LCC PZ7.B229515 Js 2019 | DDC [Fic]—dc23
LC record available at https://lccn.loc.gov/2019006071

ISBN 978-1-64375-130-6 (PB)

10 9 8 7 6 5 4 3 2 1
First Paperback Edition

For Waynie and Wendy.
And for all my Caribbean family displaced
by extreme weather. May you find home again.

1

The Horizon

Corinne La Mer leapt from one tall coconut tree to another. Nothing but air surrounded her and there was only the sand and a few sharp rocks below. She landed on the rough trunk of the tree, slapping it hard with her palms and then wrapping her legs around it. She slipped and felt a rush of panic rise to her throat until she got the soles of her feet flat against the bark to grip her in place.

Corinne looked down at the beach. Mrs. Duval, in a bright purple headwrap and a loose white blouse and colorful skirt, shaded her eyes as she peered into the tree.

"Don't injure yourself before you get my coconuts, please," she teased Corinne.

Next to Mrs. Duval was Corinne's friend Malik. He shaded his face with a small hand, watching Corinne as she moved. His older brother, Bouki, wasn't looking her way at all. He was focused on the road, hoping for one last customer before they called it a morning.

Corinne caught her breath and returned to her task. It was dizzyingly high at the top of the coconut trees. Even in the shade of their large fan-like leaves, and with the sea breeze blowing to shore, the heat had her drenched in sweat. She panted as she reached up for a thick, yellow coconut. She twisted and twisted it until the tough stem snapped and then looked down to see where Malik was waiting to catch it, but the coconut slipped from her sweat-slick palm.

"Watch out!" she cried. Malik stepped nimbly out of the way, but Bouki, busily counting Mrs. Duval's coins, didn't hear her warning. The coconut grazed the side of his arm and dropped near his foot.

"You nearly killed me!" he yelled.

"I said 'watch out.'" Corinne carefully climbed back down the sloping trunk. She had skinned the insides of her thighs climbing down before and had learned to use the soles of her feet to keep her body away from the bark. When she was close enough to the bottom, she pushed off the tree and landed near Bouki, who had lopped off the top of the coconut with a machete and passed it to Mrs. Duval.

Mrs. Duval shook the coconut and screwed up her face. "All these coconuts dry, dry these days. I thought it was rainy season already." She peered up into the tree again. "Aren't there any more up there?"

Bouki patted the trunk. "We only have what nature gives us," he said.

"And whatever else you can grab," Mrs. Duval added.

Bouki put on a fake look of offense as he pocketed her money, but it was not news to anyone that Bouki and Malik used to be thieves.

"They're reformed," Corinne said.

"Hmm. Reformed," Mrs. Duval repeated, looking at the boys out of the corner of her eye. She sniffed the opening of the coconut and first sipped, then tipped it back and drank long. When she finally came up for air, there was a look of satisfaction on her face, but only for a moment. "You should go back to selling oranges," Mrs. Duval said to Corinne. "Nothing on the island compares to your oranges."

Corinne blushed, but her gaze flitted over the waves, and the compliment faded quickly. "I can't only sell oranges, Mrs. Duval," she said. "It's not good business."

"Ah, of course," Mrs. Duval said, smiling. She turned to the beach, where a band of children played on the sand. She waved at them to catch their attention, and then pointed with the whole length of her arm to a pink house. They all went running.

Corinne waved at Laurent, the oldest of the bunch, who played cricket with her when he wasn't doing chores or watching his younger siblings.

"I can send him along later," Mrs. Duval said. "If you want to play."

Corinne shook her head. "Maybe another time."

"You know," Mrs. Duval said, leaning in close. "You can't watch the waves forever." When Corinne didn't answer, Mrs. Duval picked up all her coconuts by the stems and walked behind her children to their house.

The sea was bright blue and the sun reflected off the choppy waves in dazzling silver and gold. In the line of fishing boats near the horizon, Corinne could just make out her papa's, even though it was impossible to see its bright yellow color. She had memorized the shape of it, so she could always pick out her papa on the waves.

"He's safe, you know," Bouki said.

"For now," Corinne replied.

"You worry too much."

Corinne turned from the sea to look at her friend. There had been a time when she didn't worry. That was before her orange trees bore their first fruit, when she and her papa had their routine. He would wake her up in the morning and tell her to be careful on land, and she would tell him to mind that the sea didn't swallow him up, and they would both promise to be safe. But then

Severine came. She was beautiful at first, dreadful at their last encounter, and with her came all of the jumbies.

"You don't worry enough," Corinne told Bouki. She clutched the stone pendant of the necklace that hung near her heart, and rubbed its cracked surface with her thumb.

Corinne hadn't believed in jumbies before Severine followed her out of the forest. She thought they were only stories that grown-ups told to scare the children on the island, stories about things that came out at night so little ones would stay in their beds. But then she encountered creatures with backward feet, women who shed their skin, and men covered in spiky fur with teeth as sharp as daggers. There was a jumbie who cared for the woods, and one who lived beneath the waves who would turn anyone into stone at a glance and who ruled the mermaids in the sea. Corinne had seen them all. But worse than that, she had witnessed their power, and she understood just how easy it was to succumb to any one of them.

She had nearly lost her papa to Severine, and Bouki to Mama D'Leau. It was enough to make anyone worry.

Months ago, when Corinne had dragged Severine into the sea and left her there, she had been sure that it was only a matter of time before the sea spat Severine back out.

"The sea doesn't keep anything, Corinne," her papa had told her. So today, and every day, she stayed near the shore watching the waves and waiting.

Corinne nicked the skin of her thumb on a sharp edge of her stone necklace. The stone had been her mama's, and after Corinne had broken it, her papa had wrapped it in leather to hold it together again. In the months since, Corinne had rubbed some of the cracks smooth, but the stone did not soothe her like it used to.

"What is it we are looking for?" an old woman asked. She had appeared out of nowhere and stood next to them in the shade of the coconut tree.

"Witch!" Bouki said.

The witch picked up her walking stick and brought it down with force on Bouki's right foot. The sparse few strands of her short white hair shook with her jab.

Bouki doubled over to nurse his foot and looked daggers at the white witch, but he knew enough not to say anything else.

"Good morning, neighbor," Corinne said.

The witch knocked her walking stick on the trunk of the tree and squinted up at the fruit. "Any more good ones left?" she asked.

"All green," Corinne said.

The witch nodded. "I don't mind the young ones."

Malik scrambled up the tree. The witch leaned against the trunk, letting her stick rest against its curve. She rubbed her left arm slowly.

Everything about the white witch looked like it was near expiration: the sun-bleached pattern on her dress, the threadbare wrap that tied her head, the few drooping twists of short white hair that refused to be contained in her headwrap. Even the skin of her body sagged loose around her bones as if it might detach and crumple around her at any moment. No one knew how old the white witch was. Even the oldest people in the villages remembered her as ancient when they were young.

Corinne watched the witch massage her damaged arm. It was even more shriveled and grayer than the rest of her, as if the life had been leached out of it. But at the end of her arm, her hand seemed more vibrant. Her fingers curled and stretched in short, jerking movements.

"Your hand is getting stronger," Corinne said.

"There's only two ways for a thing to go," the witch said. "Better, or worse." She stretched and bent her fingers as she looked out to sea. "What you looking out at the sea for? You already know what is under the water."

Before Corinne could find an answer, Malik jumped to the ground holding a coconut with just the barest hint of yellow on the husk. He macheted the top off before presenting it to the witch.

The witch's tongue jumped out in anticipation, flicking over her thin, dry lips. She took the husk in her good hand and drank deeply. Some of the water dribbled out the sides of her mouth, past a patch of gray chin-stubble, and down the dark, wrinkled folds of her throat, which made jerking movements like fresh fish bundled in a net.

She downed the entire contents in one go. Then she handed the coconut back to Malik. He moved to cut it open, but she shook her head. "There's nothing there," she said. She seemed to be discussing the sea, not the lack of jelly in the coconut.

Without another word, the witch shuffled off, kicking up pale sand.

"Didn't I say that, brother?" Bouki asked. "Didn't I tell her that nothing was going to happen?"

"Is that what I said?" the witch called over her shoulder. She maneuvered back around to face them. "Dunce. Who ever said nothing is going to happen?" She lifted her cane with some difficulty and gestured around her. Her loose dress rippled in the wind. "Something is always happening." She moved her mouth in a way that made Corinne think she was rearranging her teeth before she continued. "Boy, nothing is as dull as you."

"You think something else is going to happen," Corinne said.

The witch shot her the same look of disdain she had turned on Bouki. "Something is happening right now," she said. "And a moment after that something will happen again." She cut her eyes at Bouki again. "Maybe you are spending too much time with this one. You were smarter when you were coming to the market alone. You will miss things if you keep wasting time standing guard at the sea. You think this is the only piece of shore? The only spread of water?" She stretched her ruined fingers again and muttered, "Only two ways for things to go, better or worse. And there's nothing you can do about it."

They watched the witch as she bent the corner around a grove of coconut trees. It was only after she was out of sight that Bouki shouted, "She didn't pay!"

2

The Jumbie in the Forest

In the sticky thickness of the forest, a large boulder covered with moss and slime sat precariously on a small square bit of rock. It rested at the edge of a sprawling plain in which several saplings were stretching toward the sky. If there had been any people there, they might have thought the boulder almost looked like an old man crouching, balancing on the flat of a pair of hooves where his toes should have been, and frowning over the plain. But there were no people there. No one ever went this far into the forest, because it was where most jumbies lived, hidden in the shadows.

Far above the tips of the old trees, the saplings, and the craggy stone that looked both like an old man and an old goat, the sky turned gray like hard steel. Then a few drops splattered down, swiping leaves and blades of grass, and smacking the boulder on its back.

The boulder seemed to tremble at the annoyance, and slowly unfolded itself, softening and smoothing, shaking dust and pebbles off its surface until it was a real man with hairy goat's legs. Matted gray hair entwined with moss and leaves tumbled down the man's back. Still crouched, the man looked up at the sky, slowly, as was his way. He reached a hand out, and a drop of water plopped into the center of his palm. He brought it to his wrinkled mouth and sipped.

The ancient creases of his face deepened, his jaw tightened, and his light brown eyes went a reddish color like the ground that was muddying at his hooves.

He picked up a long, thick stick lying near his feet, and used it to push himself to standing. He wasn't tall, but with his shoulders back and his chin up, he seemed as large and unmovable as the rock he had been only moments before.

Papa Bois—that was the old jumbie's name—sighed. He shook his head and a few crumbles of dirt tumbled from the strands of his hair. In the distance he heard someone plucking a quick, tripping melody on a cuatro. The music blended wonderfully with the sound of water running over rocks in the nearby river.

Papa Bois was glad his love was so close, waiting and happy for once. It was a shame he was going to give her bad news.

3

June, Too Soon

The rain began softly at first, then quickly turned into pelting droplets that slapped Corinne's skin. She put her hands over her head, but in moments, her long black braids became soaking whips that lashed her neck and chest as she ran for shelter beneath an almond tree.

People on the beach grabbed up towels and children and snacks and toys, and ran for cover. Some went straight to their brightly colored houses on the shore. Others ran to the tree line, hiding under any available branch. A couple squeezed next to the snack stall at the edge of the road, taking what little shelter they could in its propped-up awning.

The sky blackened and the wind whipped up. The same coconut trees Corinne and the boys had been climbing bowed toward the sea, pointing straight at the line of fishing boats on the churning water.

The rain dulled everything, even the shapes of the boats. Corinne could not make out her papa's.

Mind the sea doesn't swallow you up, she thought with a chill.

"We should get inside," Bouki said.

Corinne nodded. "You go back to town. I will wait here for my papa."

Bouki squinted up at the sky. "Don't wait too long."

The boys took off up the hill, and Corinne peered out at the horizon. Her heart thudded as fast as the raindrops striking the ground. From behind the gray veil of rain, the boats appeared. They were only dark shapes at first, but as they came closer the colors of each vessel, blue, green, red, and finally the bright yellow of Pierre La Mer's, came into focus.

Corinne ran to the sea. The wind pushed at her and the rain slapped against her, but she sprinted until she reached her papa.

Pierre called to her, but whatever he said was whisked away by the wind. He pointed over her head toward their little house at the top of the hill. Corinne understood, but did not stop. She met him in hip-deep water and pulled the boat from the front as her father jumped out and pushed, steering it through the choppy waves. Once on shore, they hoisted it onto soft sand. Pierre knotted a rope around one of the posts at the dock and threw a tarp over the boat for cover. Then he lashed it with more rope, pulling it taut and tying it before he turned back to Corinne.

"Come!" he shouted over the wind.

The two ran to the dirt road, past the almond tree, and up the hill to their little house.

The windows banged open and shut in the wind. A gust knocked Corinne into a patch of mud and splashed her up to the neck. She slipped back into the puddle when she tried to get her feet under her, so Pierre grabbed her work shirt to pull her out. Together they scrambled for the front door, bracing against the wind.

Corinne pulled the door open. Inside the house was a mess. The rain had blown in and left everything sodden.

Glass rattled in the wooden window frames, adding to the cacophony of the howling wind outside. They rushed to the windows, fighting wet, whipping curtains to pull the frames shut and secure each iron hook into the eye that held it closed. But the windows still shook, struggling against the hooks like creatures desperate to be free of their bonds.

In the relative stillness, Corinne and Pierre tried to catch their breath as rainwater and mud from their hair and clothes pooled at their feet.

"That came on suddenly," Corinne said between pants.

Pierre nodded. "We didn't even see the clouds. One minute, blue sky, and then the next . . . I've never seen anything like it before." A frown flickered across Pierre's face, but he smoothed it away quickly. "We should clean up."

Corinne gathered towels. She wrapped one around herself to stave off the shivering and used another to sop up the wet floors.

Pierre went through the house picking up items that had fallen to the floor. Broken wares, utensils, a tin cup. "Look, she survived," he said, holding out a small grayish wax statue of a woman.

Corinne cupped it gently in her hand and took it to her bedroom, laying it in the center of the bed, where it was safest. The wax sculpture was of her mother, and Corinne had made it herself months ago. Since then, it had broken twice. A third time, she feared, would make it irreparable.

The wind pushed rain through every crevice. Corinne and her father used towels to stop up the spaces under the doors, between the walls and the windows, and in the seams between the wall boards. By the time they were finished, the air was stifling.

And there was nothing to do but wait.

Corinne changed into a colorful skirt and white blouse, an outfit that most girls on the island wore. She only ever wore her papa's old shirts and pants when she

< 15 >

was at work. It was impossible to climb coconut trees and pick oranges in a skirt.

Outside, the plants bowed in the wind. Branches snapped, and leaves scraped against the shivering glass windows. Corinne moved into the kitchen and put some water on to boil. After she pulled a bottle of tea leaves out and put them in a strainer, she took two tin mugs out of the cupboard. When the water was ready, she poured it over the strainer and into each mug. Then she quartered an orange and squeezed juice into the tea.

The room filled with the orange's bright scent, and the warmth of the hot water penetrated straight to Corinne's bones. She brought the cups to the table, where Pierre inhaled deeply before lifting his and taking a sip. The windows rattled, and the wind and rain howled.

"We'll have to secure the windows better," he said.

"Do you think it's that bad?" she asked.

"Hurricane," he said.

"It's too early for hurricanes. June, too soon. July, stand by. August, come it must. September, remember. October, all over."

"I don't think the storm knows that poem," Pierre said. "It's definitely a hurricane." His head tilted as he listened. "It's getting quiet." The trees still trembled, but they weren't bending the way they had been minutes before. "Let's go."

Corinne didn't like the sound of Pierre's voice. It was low and gravelly, filled with worry. She downed her tea quickly and followed him out the back door.

The wind pushed against them, spattering debris against their bodies, but there was plenty of work to be done. Pierre gathered a few loose boards. While Corinne held them in place over the windows, he hammered nails into the frames. They made their way quickly around the house. When they came around to the back again, the wind seemed to have died down, but the sea was still roiling as if it was being stirred up from beneath the surface. The piece of wood Corinne was holding slipped from her hand as she watched the water, and Pierre's hammer banged straight against the window frame, shattering the glass.

"Corinne!"

"Sorry, Papa," she said. "But look at the sea!"

Every muscle in Pierre's body tightened when he looked. "There's nothing we can do about that. Like every other storm, we will have to wait it out."

But this wasn't like every other storm. It was a hurricane. In June. There was nothing normal about that. She had a sick feeling about why this hurricane was too early. What had been the cause of every strange thing on the island in recent months? The jumbies. Perhaps this was what the white witch had meant. Corinne was missing things by looking so far out to sea. The problem was in the water, just beneath her own house.

Corinne's stomach knotted.

There was always some selfish motive behind the jumbies' behavior. Corinne could find out why a hurricane was being whipped up now. But the only way was to face Mama D'Leau, the cruelest of the jumbies.

< 18 >

4

Only a Storm

Rain was nothing to Mama D'Leau. She lived for water. She ruled it. The jumbie sat on the muddy bank of the river in a thick patch of grass. Her body and arms draped over the fallen trunk of a tree, while the thick anaconda's tail that started at her waist wrapped around the other end of the tree trunk and sloped into the water. Occasionally she flicked the tip of her tail, spraying droplets in time with the music she plucked out on the cuatro strings.

As the rain came harder, Mama D'Leau turned her face to the sky and let the water roll down her throat and neck. It soaked into the long braided ropes of black hair that fell over her back and chest, hiding her nakedness. The rain thunked against the cuatro's strings and drummed on its polished wood body, adding to its music. The rain puckered the surface of the river and tapped the rocks and the leaves of the mango tree above her. Mama D'Leau tilted her head to listen, then changed her tune.

'Twas Friday morn when we set sail
And we were not far from the land
When the captain, he spied a lovely mermaid
With a comb and a glass in her hand ... her hand ...
With a comb and a glass in her hand ...

Her voice was soft as she twined the lyrics with the percussion of the rain.

"Beauty," said Papa Bois.

Mama D'Leau let her last note trail off and turned to see the old jumbie emerge near a wild-growing okra plant. Her face, already soft from singing, relaxed even more. Papa Bois smiled deeply.

"Ah *oui*," said Mama D'Leau. "And what it is you want now?"

Papa Bois pointed at the sky and squinted up at the rain. "Do you feel that?" he asked.

"What is it I should feel, eh?" Mama D'Leau sucked her teeth, *chups*. "You always worrying about something."

"And you not worrying enough," Papa Bois said

gently. He held his hand out and let the raindrops dance in his palm.

Mama D'Leau frowned. She stuck her tongue out and tasted the storm. Her eyes flashed the same gray color as the rainwater and her tail coiled tightly under her as if she was getting ready to spring.

Papa Bois moved closer, and Mama D'Leau tilted her body to block a little nest she had made surrounding a small opal that looked like the bottom of the ocean. She palmed it, pulling the opal to her chest as she turned away from Papa Bois.

"I see it already. No point trying to hide it now," he drawled.

Mama D'Leau opened her palm just enough for the stone to shine in her hand. There was a small nick in the side that she rubbed gently. Every time she did, she thought of the irritating boy who had marred its perfect surface. "It has nothing to do with this," she said. "I've had it for months already. You didn't think of that, eh?" She looked smugly at him, but only for a moment.

Papa Bois took a breath as slow as a flower opening at dawn. "Something is coming," he said.

"It is only a storm, love," she said, but her words were edged with worry.

"No, *doux doux*. Not only that."

Mama D'Leau unwrapped herself from the broken tree trunk. She gripped the stone more tightly and slithered into the water as the rain beat down all around her. Beneath the ruffled surface, she watched Papa Bois walk to where she had been and pick up the cuatro she left behind. He embraced the instrument, holding it against his bare chest, then returned slowly to the forest. Only then, Mama D'Leau left.

5

Summon the Sea

By late afternoon, the oil lamps were nearly empty. They swayed on their hooks in the kitchen each time wind rocked the house. Corinne watched their flames burn down to low orange glows, like sunsets. Then they went dark and everything became still. Despite the fact they were far from sunset, the house was as black as midnight.

"Hear that?" Pierre asked.

"The rain is dying down," she said.

Pierre took three long strides to the back of the kitchen and carefully opened the top of the Dutch door. A fine mist blew inside, sprinkling the wooden floor like flour from a sifter.

"Is it over, Papa?" Corinne asked.

"It's only the eye of the storm," he answered. "The wind and rain will come again. We don't have much time." He stepped into the yard and beckoned to her. "Come."

The thick cloud cover surrounded them like a pouch that could close in at any moment. And beneath it, the brown sea writhed. The beach was strewn with debris. Torn-off coconut leaves, broken branches, and seaweed littered the sand. A sunbeam, like a long, thin finger, pushed through a hole in the knitted clouds, illuminating a single spot in the middle of the sea. The air was still and heat pressed around Corinne like a hand around a throat. How much time did she have in the eye of a storm?

As Pierre began to drag broken branches away from the side of the house, Corinne snuck down to the sea.

The hill was slick with reddish mud that ran in thick rivulets. Corinne skidded and stubbed her toe on rocks and tree roots, but she kept moving. Nothing was going to stop her now. At the bottom of the hill the beach sand was a minefield of broken, jagged shells and rocks and sodden pits of mud. She tried to pick her way through, but the sand sucked at her feet, sinking her to her ankles with every step. She lost one sandal and then another as she pulled her feet out of the muck, but she was determined to reach the edge of the waves. Above her, the clouds began to close in.

It was time to call the jumbie.

The first time Corinne had faced Mama D'Leau, she had been armed with offerings, things that would make the jumbie talk, things that would please her. She had been warned to never ask a question. And she had had the support of her friends. Corinne had never faced Mama D'Leau alone. But she knew that the storm would only dredge the worst things to the surface—just like after the earthquake, when children all over the island began to go missing.

Corinne opened and closed her empty hands and steeled herself to the possibility that she would face the jumbie's wrath. She got ready to beg. She had nothing else to give.

The wind picked up again and pushed Corinne's braids out of her face and her blouse against her chest. She leaned into the air and made it to the mucky edge of the waves that deposited small pieces of wood, shell, and weeds on her bare toes.

"Mama!" she called into the waves.

The wind pulled her voice back and pushed at her as if it was trying to keep her away from the sea.

"Mama!" Corinne screamed. "I need you!"

Corinne understood the rules. The white witch had been very clear about them. Without an offering from Corinne, the jumbie was unlikely to show herself, but this was not the usual situation.

The surface of the water smoothed as if someone had pulled a wrinkled sheet tight across a bed and tucked in the edges. Corinne entered the water. She remembered her own mama's hands, brown and smooth and warm. She clutched her necklace, squeezing the stone her mama had left for her. It had saved her twice now. But she didn't know if it had anything left to give.

She whispered "Mama" again, only this time she tried to picture her own mother's face. She struggled to pick out any individual feature like the crook of her smile or the wideness of her eyes. Pierre described Corinne's mother, Nicole, to her often, but lately, Corinne couldn't summon her mother's features. They blurred like a dream that had faded. Corinne held the stone pendant out. What else did she have to offer? "Mama, please," she said. Her throat and eyes began to burn. Corinne stumbled as the sharp, splintered edges of coconut husks, twigs, and leaves scratched at her legs.

She shut her eyes.

A wet hand cupped her cheek, as if to comfort her, but the fingers were ice cold. When Corinne looked up, she was gazing into the face of Mama D'Leau. The jumbie's eyes were brown with clouds of golden sand, the same as the sea, and they were hard as stones.

Mama D'Leau's deep brown skin glistened from the sea-water, catching what little light filtered through the thick clouds. Her long braided hair, usually perfectly neat and wrapped on the top of her head, fell around her shoulders like frayed rope. Not a crab or snail twined its way through her strands, and instead of fresh coral and bright seaweed, dull, broken sticks and rotting kelp tangled in her hair. The plaits ended past her waist, where her thick, tough anaconda tail began. Its muscles moved in a slow undulation as Mama D'Leau towered over Corinne, while the thin end of it flicked sand-stirred water into Corinne's face.

Mama D'Leau's sharp nails traced a line down from Corinne's cheek. When she came to the necklace, the jumbie wrapped her fingers around the stone and yanked it, breaking the cord from Corinne's neck. "What you want now?" Mama D'Leau asked. "You can't see I busy?"

Corinne gritted her teeth. She had been right. Mama D'Leau was to blame for the storm. Corinne resisted the urge to rub the burning spot where the necklace snapped. She didn't want to give Mama D'Leau the satisfaction of knowing she was hurt. "I want you to stop," Corinne said, careful not to ask any questions. "You have everything you asked for. There is no reason to do this."

"I?" Mama D'Leau said. "You think I cause this storm?" She sucked her teeth, *chups*. "You realize this is the second time you blame me for something I didn't cause?"

"You made the tidal wave that knocked Severine from under the rocks," Corinne said. "And you are whipping up the sea now. No one else could do it."

Mama D'Leau sat back on the coils of her tail. They slithered in circles beneath her. "Is that so?" She folded her arms. "The question, I suppose, is why you think I doing all that."

"Because you want me to run another errand for you," Corinne said. "You needed that opal." Corinne took a tentative step farther into the sea. "But now that you have it, there isn't anything else I can do for you." Corinne looked around, worried at the state of the sea. "I fulfilled my end of the bargain."

Mama D'Leau's eyes flashed like lightning, and her face was nose to nose with Corinne's in an instant. "Not entirely," she growled. "You brought me the stone, but you didn't do *everything* I asked."

Corinne stepped back. Her heart roiled like the sea around her. "Ellie," she whispered, shuddering as she remembered the mermaid that had been lost. "I . . . I . . ." she said.

Mama D'Leau waved a hand and turned away. She picked up a long, dull braid and twisted it around her fingers.

Corinne had seen Dru play with her hair before when she was nervous.

"So . . . you didn't do this," Corinne said.

"Corinne!" Pierre called from the beach.

"It's all right, Papa," Corinne said. "It really is just a storm."

Pierre threw a heated look at Mama D'Leau as he rushed to Corinne's side and pulled her back to shore.

"Papa!" Corinne protested.

"I told you there wasn't much time," Pierre thundered.

"I told you the storm would be back. It's dangerous, Corinne. You could be killed."

What little light there was around them dimmed as he spoke. The sea dulled to a murky gray and the clouds over their heads tightened. Rain hurtled at them in huge drops.

Mama D'Leau looked to the sky and shuddered.

The relief Corinne had felt only moments before evaporated in the warm air. She followed Mama D'Leau's gaze into the clouds. A bolt of lightning cracked against the gray.

Mama D'Leau covered her head with her arms.

"We have to get off the wet sand, Corinne," Pierre said. His face looked nearly as stricken as Mama D'Leau's.

"What is it, Papa?" she asked.

"Lightning doesn't come with hurricanes," he said. "Not often, anyway. I've only seen this once before."

"You said you'd never seen a storm like this one, Papa."

Pierre's only response was grabbing Corinne's hands in his own and pulling her away from the sea.

"When?" Corinne asked.

Pierre kept moving and did not answer. As they retreated, Victor, one of the fishermen from the village, ran toward the sea. His muscles rippled with effort as he tore toward the edge of the waves.

In his hands was a long fishing spear, and in his eyes was a look of determination and rage.

6

Blood in the Water

Victor grunted as he hurled the spear. Its sharpened tip gleamed as he launched it at Mama D'Leau. The jumbie twisted left, just out of the way, and grabbed the shaft with her right hand, but the spear had met its mark. It stabbed one of the coils of her tail and vibrated in her flesh.

Mama D'Leau and Corinne both screamed. The jumbie pulled at the spear, but its hook was designed to keep fish lodged in place. She wrapped the end of her tail around the wooden shaft and broke it off, but the tip remained firmly in place.

Corinne slipped out of Pierre's grasp and skidded

on the wet sand as she ran back toward the jumbie. She moved into the water, just as another bolt of lightning tore across the sky and shot into the waves. Debris hit her face and body and the stirred-up sand obstructed her view. She couldn't see anything beyond the reach of her hands.

The jumbie writhed in the water. The force of her tail whipping wildly sent more sand and bubbles into Corinne's eyes. One strong pulse tumbled Corinne backward. When she crashed into the seafloor, she had no idea how far she had been pushed. Her lungs burned for air. She swam for the surface. Both the island and Mama D'Leau were farther away than she had hoped, and with the rain coming down again, the surface of the water was rough and hard to navigate. She kept her eyes on the jumbie and swam. When she was close enough she dove again. Even in the dim light she could see a cloud of thick, red blood trailing from Mama D'Leau's tail. Corinne followed it, trying to get her hands on the spear.

What you doing? Mama D'Leau's voice came strong and clear under the water, even though the jumbie never moved her mouth.

Don't move, Corinne thought.

The jumbie slowed her movements enough for Corinne to get in closer. With every attempt Corinne made to pull the hook, Mama D'Leau's muscled tail trembled and more blood erupted, clouding Corinne's vision. She didn't have the strength to pry the hook free. She surfaced again for another breath and dove to the spear again. This time, another pair of brown arms wrapped themselves around Mama D'Leau's tail. Corinne's papa had come. He held the jumbie steady and helped Corinne rock the spear back and forth until both the pointed tip and the curved hook had come free.

White flesh stuck to the edges of the spear and another flood of dark blood came with it. Corinne and Pierre pushed for the surface, leaving the spear to fall to the bottom of the sea.

The rain poured so hard they could barely see land. It was only the flicker of lamplight, like fireflies in the distance, that gave them direction. Pierre grabbed the back of Corinne's shirt and pulled her along as he swam. He was the strongest swimmer Corinne knew, but when she looked at the shore after a time, it seemed no closer. Pierre took a deep breath and was about to start swimming again when something thick and tough shoved them, sending them tumbling to the edge of the water in an instant. They crawled to shore, spitting up sand and seawater. Victor glared mutely at them.

Pierre picked Corinne up and ran for the hill. As she looked back, something in the clouds caught her eye. A dark shape took form, billowing and moving with the wind. It looked like a man at first, standing with his hands on his hips and his legs extending toward the sea. One of his legs looked like the long, slender tail of a fish, ending in a fin where a foot should have been. Then the dark clouds of the body rearranged themselves into a face. Lightning flashed, brightening the flat nose and cruel mouth, and sparkling in the wide-set eyes, making them sharp with rage, looking right at Corinne. Just as Corinne was about to show her papa, the clouds rearranged and the man was gone.

Once they were inside the house, Pierre released Corinne from his grasp and panted. "Why would you do that?" he shouted. "Why?"

Corinne was frozen to the spot. Her papa had never raised his voice like this before. Her throat felt thick and her chest burned. She opened her mouth to explain, but couldn't think of what to say.

"You left the house in a storm. You went into the water when lightning was flashing. You know better than this, Corinne."

"Yes, Papa," she said. "I'm sorry."

"Sometimes you don't think things through, Corinne. You just do them." He dropped his body into the nearest chair and his head into the palms of his hands. "You keep putting yourself in danger. You will get hurt."

Corinne twisted the hem of her work shirt.

"I'm sorry," Pierre said. He got up and brought towels for them. He draped one over his shoulders and sopped Corinne's wet hair with another. "I know you wouldn't have gone out there unless you thought it was necessary."

"No, Papa."

"This is not the first time you have decided to do something without telling me."

"I know, Papa."

"So maybe this time you can let me know what's going on," he said. "Maybe I can even help." He undid Corinne's plaits. "What is it?"

"I think Severine is back."

"You saw her?" Pierre asked, stiffening.

"No, Papa. Not yet. But this storm came on fast, and the sea has never looked like that. I thought it was Mama D'Leau making trouble at first, but then she looked so frightened. I knew it had to be Severine."

"First you thought it was Mama D'Leau and now you're sure it's Severine." Pierre frowned. "The storm is unusual," he said. "I don't have an explanation for why it happened so suddenly, or why there is lightning. But we have had storms before."

"This bad?" Corinne asked.

Pierre's jaw tightened. "Worse." His voice was barely a whisper. He turned away, dipping his head under his own towel. He seemed to be wiping his eyes, but Corinne couldn't be sure.

"And you survived," Corinne said.

This time she saw his shoulders slump just slightly before he answered, "I did. But nothing is a guarantee, Corinne. Nature is more dangerous than any jumbie. Do you understand?"

Corinne's throat closed up. Her papa didn't believe her. She couldn't find the words to argue.

"Stay close," he said. "Promise."

She nodded.

All night, the storm raged even more loudly than it had before the eye. Corinne huddled in the middle of the kitchen of the little house on the hill while the wind howled around them, prying at the boards they had nailed over the windows. The nails squeaked against the wood and the boards groaned with every gust. Pierre paced the house, frowning. When the lamps ran out of oil and the flames dulled and went out in a whimper of smoke, Corinne dragged herself to bed and tried to sleep.

She stared at the ceiling as little white wood lizards darted up the walls and over her head, stopping every time the house shook. She wanted to tell them it would be all right, but the truth was, she wasn't so sure. Her mind was filled with the images of Mama D'Leau bleeding in agony under the water, Victor's angry face as he hurled the spear, and the man in the clouds that seemed to be looking down at the island with eyes bright as lightning.

7

The Crying Bride

Sunlight slashed through the slats of wood nailed to Corinne's bedroom window and forced her awake, but it was like swimming to the surface from fathoms below. When she finally blinked her eyes open, dust motes danced in the thin cuts of light. Everything smelled damp and fresh. She turned and swung her feet off the bed.

In the outer rooms, the windows had already been opened, and Corinne squinted in bright light. She went to the kitchen with her nightgown flapping around her knees and heard hammering from outside. She pushed her feet into a pair of old leather slippers at the door to follow the sound.

At the horizon, the sea was bright and beautiful, but nearer to shore, where the water was still stirred up from the storm, it remained a dull brown, a little darker than the sand. People were already out, picking through the muck, gathering up planks of wood and bits of galvanized roofs that had blown off their homes. The sound of waves crashing was punctuated by the calls of mothers below, warning small children to be careful as they wound their way across the beach.

Corinne chilled. Months ago, she had seen the same scene, but with mothers calling for their missing children after the earthquake. She tensed.

Pierre stopped his work. "It's all right," he said. "Everyone is accounted for."

Corinne felt some relief, but she couldn't relax entirely. She turned to the potted plants that had fallen over near the back door. The ceramic was broken and sodden soil spilled across the damp grass. Corinne rocked the pepper plant upright and packed as much soil back into the damaged pot as it would hold. Then she turned to the other uprooted plants nearby. It looked as if the wind had curled fingers around each one and plucked them from the ground, leaving their roots exposed and baking in the sun. At the front of the house, several oranges had rolled in the dirt around the yard. Corinne gathered them up in the hem of her nightgown, carried them inside, and emptied them into the sink.

Pierre followed her in. "Corinne," he said. "I know I was harsh with you last night. What you did was dangerous. The island hasn't seen a storm like this in a long time." He looked at her gently. "You wouldn't remember. You were just starting to walk. And we lost so much, Corinne." He rubbed his hand on the back of her head. "There is so much to lose."

"I understand, Papa," Corinne said. But she saw something like pain flash across his face. He wasn't hurt over the broken windows and the uprooted plants. There was something else bothering him, something worse. "The storm is over, Papa," she continued. "There is nothing to worry about."

But Pierre's expression didn't alter. Whatever was on his mind, he wouldn't say.

Once the yard had been cleaned up, Corinne headed to town. Much of the dirt road was washed away. Mud still flowed down the sides, spilling over rocks and broken wood, and burying leaves and the remains of fruit. Corinne hopped through the ruined path, slipping and skidding as she went. By the time she reached Hugo's bakery, she was splashed in mud to her knees. Bouki and Malik waved her in through the front door.

"Take off your sandals," Bouki said.

"When did you get so domesticated?" Corinne asked.

"You can't track mud into a place with food. Everybody knows that."

Corinne smiled and took off her shoes to go inside.

Hugo pushed past a beaded curtain. His face brightened when he spotted Corinne. "I was wondering how long it would take you to get here," he said. "How is your papa? And the house?"

"We didn't take too much damage," Corinne said. "Papa is fixing some of the broken windows. How was it here?"

"We're in a good spot," Bouki declared.

Corinne suppressed a giggle. Not a few months ago, the brothers had lived in the caves in the foothills of a mountain. They had never wanted to live in a house, even one in a "good spot" like Hugo's.

"Are you hungry, Corinne?" Hugo asked.

She shook her head. "I was just checking on you on my way—"

"To see Dru?" Bouki finished.

Malik looked up the road and shook his head.

"Be careful," Hugo said. "Some places really took a beating."

Corinne left the boys and Hugo and took the curving road toward Dru's village. In several places, the path was cut off by fallen trees. It was a good thing Corinne had chosen her work clothes—a pair of her papa's old pants rolled to her calves and an old shirt pushed up to her elbows—for the trek. She couldn't possibly have traversed the muck in anything else. She scrambled over a tree trunk that lay across the market road and landed on the other side in a patch of leaves. With her next step, she heard a tiny squeak. She lifted her foot and a mouse no bigger than her thumb shot out of the pile of leaves and made for the forest. After that, Corinne moved more carefully, flicking away leaves with her toes before she stepped down to make sure she didn't squish some other small creature. It made the going slow.

When she turned on the road that went past the cane fields, there were no fallen trees, and the gravelly road was easier to navigate.

Most of the sugarcane had survived. Some of it was bent or broken at the edges of the field. The cane in the center still held up tall and strong. The field toward the back was where Dru's family worked, so Corinne was glad it still looked in good condition. But when she came to the entrance to Dru's village, she froze.

The houses in Dru's village had never been sturdy. They were a collection of wood planks built on hard-packed clay, held together with screws and galvanized roofing that were sometimes also used as walls. Rust had eaten through some of the houses on their best day, but now the structures sagged and leaned and looked about to collapse.

There were black flies everywhere, buzzing in patches over the carcasses of animals that hadn't made it through the storm. In the gutter at the side of the road were a few fish, and up ahead was a bird that looked like it had fallen right out of the sky. Corinne gave each of them a wide berth.

She spotted Mrs. Ramdeen standing outside her house with her hands on her hips, her head tilted at almost the same precarious angle as the front steps to her house. A small boy appeared in the doorway, and Mrs. Ramdeen's hands flew up. "Don't stand on those, Allan!"

"Yes, Mama," Allan said. He took a flying jump from the doorway into a patch of mud, which splashed him to his thighs and little brown shorts.

"Hi, Allan," Corinne said.

"Corinne," said Mrs. Ramdeen. "What are you doing so far from home? How did your house hold up?"

"Okay. I'm looking for Dru."

Mrs. Ramdeen waved in the general direction of the rest of the village, which was strewn with boards. "Everybody is scattered, trying to salvage what they can from the mess."

"I can help you," Corinne offered.

"No," she said. "You go find your friend. The whole family is probably at the wedding tent."

Corinne was sure the bamboo tent would have been knocked flat. But if they were attending to the tent, then maybe the Rootsinghs' house was fine.

"I'm going too, Mama," Allan said.

Mrs. Ramdeen stood with her hands on her hips and grunted in response. Corinne and Allan took that as a yes.

They moved through the banging and sawing of repair work, noisy children, and scolding parents. The noise dimmed for just a moment or two as people recognized Corinne and paused. She was used to this. Ever since Severine had showed up in the village and people found out that the jumbie had been Corinne's mother's sister, Corinne had gotten sideways glances. Categorizing each stare became a game. There were three main varieties: suspicious, curious, and fearful. Corinne was still learning how to ignore the way each one made her feel small, but she combated that in the only way she could. She smiled and said, "Good morning," but not everyone responded in kind.

Allan wriggled his fingers into Corinne's hand and waved brightly at everyone. By the time they got to the end of the road, Corinne was waving, too. She was just about to thank Allan for walking with her when they heard someone crying.

She followed the noise to what was left of the bamboo tent that had been put up for the wedding of Dru's eldest sibling, Fatima. Allan pulled away and went running into the half-fallen structure. The white tarp sagged to one side and was covered in mud. At the other side, bamboo was piled at angles like a fallen wicket. In the middle of the rubble, Fatima stood crying into the end of a blue sari. Allan ran around her, hopping over the bamboo and crawling under the ripped tarp.

Fatima turned to watch him, paused her crying for a moment, then started again, louder than before.

"She's been like this all day and all night," Dru said, sidling up to Corinne. Dru tucked her shoulder-length hair behind her ears. It was cut in a straight, blunt line that grazed her shoulder blades, an improvement over the shaggy edges she had worn the last few months. The hem of her yellow kurta was muddy, and there were flecks of dirt on her face and pieces of leaves in her hair.

"Your house doesn't look too bad," Corinne said, gazing back down the road.

Dru's eyes widened. "I thought the whole thing would fall in on us. The walls rattled all night. The goats crawled under the house and cried until everything stopped. It was impossible to sleep."

Corinne looked from Dru to her sister, to the mama goat and kids that were bounding through the bamboo with Allan. "Who was louder? Fatima or the goats?"

"Who do you think?" Dru asked.

As if on cue, Fatima wailed. The younger girls burst out laughing and Fatima cut an eye at them.

"You just wait until one of you grows up and gets married!" Fatima yelled. "I'll be sure to laugh at you then! I hope there's a storm, too, that blows down your whole wedding tent." She began to cry again.

Dru and Corinne tiptoed away.

"I'm glad you're all okay," Corinne said.

"And you?" Dru asked. "Things must be worse close to the sea."

"The house is fine."

"But?" Dru prodded.

Corinne leaned in and whispered, "I went to the sea. I saw Mama D'Leau."

"She came out?"

"I called her."

Dru shuddered. "Why?"

"I thought she had something to do with all this."

Dru took a breath and put both arms on Corinne's shoulders. "You have been looking out to sea for months." She glanced up at the sky. "This had nothing to do with the sea."

Corinne nodded. "I know. You're right."

Dru's mouth dropped open and her eyebrows shot up high.

"Don't look so surprised."

"I'm not used to you being anything but stubborn once you get an idea in your head," Dru said. Then she squinted at Corinne. "How come you agreed with me so fast? What happened when you saw Mama D'Leau?"

"She was afraid," Corinne said. "But what could frighten a jumbie?"

8

Not a Jumbie

"Are you two going to stand there all day?" Mrs. Rootsingh passed the girls, carrying a basket on her head. "Come and help, unless you want to listen to Fatima bawl forever and ever."

Corinne and Dru got to work rebuilding the tent for Fatima's wedding. They gathered bamboo poles and put them on the side so they could be re-posted and tied to the canopy. Allan gathered the ropes that had blown away. He was well suited for it because he could fit into small spaces and didn't mind digging in the mud. Every time he found one, he held it up, grinning.

Once all the poles had been piled up, Corinne looked around for something else to do.

"You have done enough," Mrs. Rootsingh said. She brushed a long strand of black hair from her face and lashed two of the bamboo poles together with rope.

"I can still help," Corinne said.

Mrs. Rootsingh flashed her eyes at Dru and then cocked an eyebrow.

Dru took Corinne's hand and pulled her away. "I think we're in the way." She tugged Corinne down the road that led to the heart of the village.

Corinne dragged her feet the entire time. Dru stopped. "You're scared of the village," she said.

"What am I afraid of?" Corinne asked.

"You're hiding. You haven't been to the market in days! Weeds are growing up in your spot."

"I've been doing other things."

"Like?"

"Selling coconuts with Bouki and Malik."

"They don't need you to sell coconuts," Dru said. "And you don't need them to sell anything."

"I left Severine in the sea," Corinne said. "And she's going to figure it out someday. Then she will be back."

"You think that the storm will make that happen? You left her across the whole ocean," Dru said. "It's a long way back."

"But not an impossible way back," Corinne said. "I returned, didn't I?"

"Yes, but you had help," Dru pointed out. "If your papa and Mama D'Leau had not come for you, maybe you wouldn't have found your way home. And anyway, look, the storm is over and nothing has happened."

It was true. The sky was bright. The clouds were moving quickly, gathering into shapes as they moved. There was one that looked like a dog or a goat that turned into a chair and then a long flower before blurring to nothing at all. Her mind went to the man she had seen in the clouds. Maybe it was nothing, but Corinne felt something in her stomach tighten. "Mama D'Leau was looking up at the sky, and her face was worried."

"It was a bad storm," Dru said. "Maybe she hasn't seen one like it in a long time."

"I don't know," Corinne said. "She must have seen so many of them." She looked around at the mud that ran down the sides of the road. "Mama D'Leau can control the currents. She can go anywhere she wants in the sea. Why would one storm bother her?"

The clouds had gone gray at the edges. She squinted, trying to make out the man again.

"What is it?" Dru asked.

"There's something else," Corinne said. "I saw something in the clouds. A person. Not exactly a person. The shape of a person. And then it turned into an angry face."

"That's nothing," Dru said. "I see things in the clouds all the time."

Corinne bit her lip. Dru was right, of course. And yet there was something Corinne was feeling that she couldn't quite explain. She moved to a nearby mango tree and sat against the trunk. Several fruits had been pried free in the storm and littered the ground at her feet. The flies had already gotten to the ripe ones. The green ones had rolled around in the dirt.

Dru sat next to her.

"Nobody believed me when I said that Severine had come back. You didn't."

Dru looked guilty.

"I'm not mad," Corinne added quickly. "It's just . . . I'm not sure what I saw wasn't real."

"But there's no jumbie that lives in the clouds," Dru said.

"It's not a jumbie!" Bouki said. He appeared next to the tree with Malik alongside.

"What do you mean?" Corinne asked.

"Maybe what you saw in the clouds wasn't a jumbie," Bouki said.

Malik's eyebrows waggled up and down as if that was explanation enough. The girls looked at each other and then back at the brothers.

"What was it then?" Dru asked.

"A god." Bouki's face was grim and Malik nodded gravely.

"That's ridiculous," Corinne said. "Gods don't pop up in the clouds!"

"Not very long ago you thought there were no such things as jumbies," Bouki said. "You don't know everything."

"Then what god is this, and why would Mama D'Leau be so afraid?" Corinne asked.

"It's the god of storms," Bouki explained. Malik trickled his fingers down like rain. "This god can break mountains, rip up forests, and flatten everything else." Malik punched his own fist and stamped his feet. "When he rages, the sea trembles, the ground, even the sky." Malik shook his hands down from the ground to up in the air.

"How do you know about this?" Corinne asked.

"Everybody knows!"

"I don't," Corinne and Dru said together.

"Are you sure?" Corinne asked.

Malik shook his head and pointed up at the sky. In the time they had been talking, the clouds had darkened again and tumbled over their heads.

The girls picked themselves up and moved beyond the tree's canopy to get a better look.

"Last night when the lightning flashed across the sky, I saw the outline of a man watching over the island in the clouds," Bouki said. "I remembered the story then, but I wasn't sure it was real until the clouds began to gather again."

Malik nodded enthusiastically.

"You know this story, too?" Corinne asked.

"Of course he does!" Bouki said. "Why would I know it and he wouldn't?"

The wind picked up and the clouds formed and re-formed into angry faces with piercing eyes and hungry mouths. The four of them shivered. Lightning flashed again and the air itself crackled.

Around the village, people paused their work to look up at the sky. Their faces were long with dread and their bodies still crouched from working. They all felt the air change. Another storm was coming.

"We can't stay here," Bouki said.

Corinne looked at the already damaged village. "Where can we go?" she asked.

Malik pointed toward the hills in the distance.

"The mountains," Bouki said. "They're solid rock, and we lived there for years. The caves have enough room for everyone."

"What about my papa and Hugo?" Corinne asked.

"When you've lived out in the open for a long time, you learn to recognize when the weather is about to take a turn," Bouki said. "As soon as we felt the air change, we told Hugo to meet us at the base of the hill with Pierre. But we have to go *now*."

The leaves of the mango tree rustled. The wind sent the hem of Dru's kurta flying into her face. Corinne's plaits whipped behind her. In the houses, curtains peeled out of windows one by one, as if the wind was taking its time going down the alley. Leaves, bits of cloth, and a little rubber ball tumbled in the muddy road. The wind pushed against everything, sending skirts and shirts flapping, and dirt and leaves scattering. Dru and Corinne let it push them back to the tent and told everyone about the plan to go to the mountains. Mrs. Rootsingh filled a water jug and wrapped a cloth around her head, then put the jug on top, holding it with one hand as she beckoned her children with the other. Mr. Rootsingh put roti skins in a paper sack and shoved the sack in a larger cloth bag that was already bulging with other supplies. Dru's siblings scattered, grabbing supplies. Arjun got a length of rope. Vidia and Karma, the two girls just older than Dru, got some more of the food. Fatima finally stopped complaining long enough to carry a jug of water, though not on her head like her mother. Then they all turned back to the road and pushed against the wind and the light rain it had brought with it.

"What about the goats?" Dru asked when they reached the boys.

"My life is ruined and you are worried about three goats?" Fatima cried.

"I'm not leaving them."

"We have to go," Bouki said.

"It won't take long to get them," Dru promised. "I can catch up." She turned and ran back to the house.

At one look from Mrs. Rootsingh, Corinne ran off after Dru. Even if Mrs. Rootsingh had not given her the eye, she wouldn't have left her friend on her own, even for a moment. She met Dru as she crawled under the house and grabbed the rope that encircled the mama goat's neck.

"Come on, come on!" Dru called.

The goat bleated, but dug its hooves into the soft ground and pulled back the other way.

Corinne crawled next to Dru and grabbed the goat by the neck. Its deep brown eyes were wide and its ears strained back. "We're trying to save you," Corinne said gently. "Come on, now."

"Get the babies," Dru said.

Corinne turned her attention to the two kids next to the mama goat. She had to crawl farther under the house, but she got her arm around one kid's neck and pulled it out. The mama charged at Corinne, and Dru yanked the rope, keeping Corinne a mere inch from a head-butting. Dru put all her weight into pulling the nanny goat away, until it stopped fighting and followed the kid that Corinne

< 52 >

had wrestled out. The second kid bounded out, skipping as if it was all a game.

Dru scowled at the goats and then down at her mud-plastered clothes.

"Well, they came out, didn't they?" Corinne said. "Come on."

The village had emptied and was silent. By the time they got to the edge of the road where it split, going one way toward the market and the other back to Dru's village, only Mr. and Mrs. Rootsingh were left. Ahead was a trail of gravel and rocks. Their neighbors were already making their way past the cane fields. Mr. Rootsingh took the mother goat's rope and led it. Mrs. Rootsingh pursed her lips when she saw Dru, but said nothing. They caught up with their neighbors just as the cane fields gave way to low, undulating rocks on the foothills toward the mountains.

Corinne and Dru pushed ahead until they caught up to Bouki and Malik, who were leading everyone up.

"Have my papa and Hugo made it yet?" Corinne asked.

Bouki shook his head.

There were more than just the Rootsinghs' neighbors picking their way through the rocks. Corinne recognized people from the market who lived in town, but she saw no one from her fishing village.

"My village is farther away. They'll come along soon," Corinne said, though it felt more like she was saying it for herself than to anyone in particular. She moved to a higher rock and strained her neck looking over each face.

"You can't wait there all day," Bouki said. "You're right. They'll catch up."

"I'll wait," Corinne said. "We can follow behind. Just be sure you know what you're doing."

Bouki made a face at her that said both *of course* and *are you kidding me?* Malik rolled his eyes and shook his head at her, as if she should have known better than to ask.

"When you lived in the mountains, you always needed to come down to town to steal things," Corinne pointed out.

"But we lived without your fancy houses and your soft blankets and your regular meals," Bouki replied.

"And this god," Corinne said.

"What about him?" Bouki asked.

"You said he could flatten mountains."

Bouki gaped, but recovered quickly. "So what?"

"Maybe the mountains aren't the best place to wait out the storm."

"Where else would you like to go?" Bouki asked. "Not all of us can turn jumbie and hide under the sea."

Corinne bit her lip. "I'm only asking if you're sure we will be safe."

"It's the safest place I know," he said.

"There!" Corinne shouted. Pierre and Hugo appeared on the market road and turned toward the rock-filled path. They were helping some older neighbors who moved

< 54 >

much more slowly. Hugo was laden with bags but still managed to help a gray-haired old man move through the rocks.

Corinne waved and Pierre waved back, then held his palm out, indicating she should wait there. She jumped off the rock near Bouki and Malik.

"Bouki?" she said.

"What now?"

"Does this god have a name?"

Malik looked at her with eyes as big as saucers. He took a long, slow breath and said, "Huracan."

9

The Way Up

More and more people joined the climb to higher ground. Families from surrounding villages— carrying small packs filled with food and water, or with babies wrapped against their parents' bodies and toddlers just able to walk on their own but needing a hand to hold—all converged on the foot of the mountain.

When Pierre and Hugo got close, Corinne joined them, helping those at the back of the crowd.

A little girl with a head full of beaded braids got her foot caught between two boulders. She managed to pull herself free, but lost her sandal. She peered into the shadowed space between the rocks. The beads on the end of her hair clicked softly around her face, but she didn't attempt a rescue.

"I'll get it," Corinne offered. She pushed her hand between the stones and freed the leather shoe, which was etched with the girl's name. "Maya?" she asked. When the girl nodded, she helped buckle it back around her ankle. "Here you go."

Maya ran to catch up with her mother, who was struggling with two even smaller children.

"What if there was a scorpion?" Dru asked. She was holding on to the mother goat's rope again, and the two little ones were bounding over the rocks, skipping ahead, and bleating joyfully even in the rain. "Or a snake!"

"She'd have a hard time without her shoe," Corinne said.

"I would have gotten a stick," Dru said. "Or found someone who could pry the rocks apart."

Corinne's steps immediately slowed. Her stomach felt sour and her head ached. She let Dru get farther up ahead before she resumed her pace. Around her the faces were all creased with concern, and dripping with rainwater. In each of those faces she saw the worry of her papa, which had deepened in the last few months after the arrival of the beautiful stranger, Severine, who turned out to be a jumbie and the sister of Corinne's mama, Nicole. Everything had been different since her aunt Severine's arrival. Their lives seemed haunted by ghosts and the ever-present idea that some new jumbie would wind up on their doorstep.

Corinne sometimes worried that she was the one who had called all the trouble to the island. It was she who had run into the forest and awakened Severine's interest. It was she who had volunteered to face Mama D'Leau. It was she who had turned into a mermaid and forced Severine into the coldest depths of water on the planet. Every time, the trouble she had tried to fix turned worse, and all because she didn't often think before she acted. Her papa had said so, and now Dru.

Going to the caves was not her plan. This time she was following. This time she couldn't be blamed if something went wrong.

The sound of sandals scraping against the rocks and swishing through the wet grass beat out an even rhythm like chac-chacs. Corinne remembered a sunny day when she rocked in a hammock in the yard while her mama looked down on her. A song wound its way up through her memory, but it was not her mama's voice she heard. It was Pierre's deep tone that carried the tune, singing to soothe her worries when the light grew dim.

"Tingalayo," Corinne sang. The sandals scraped. "Come little donkey, come."

Maya turned to look, and pulled the thumb she was sucking out of her mouth. "Tingalayo!" she sang, smiling her few milk teeth at Corinne.

"Come little donkey, come," Corinne answered. Several other children joined in.

Mih donkey walk, mih donkey talk
Mih donkey eat with a knife and fork
Mih donkey walk, mih donkey talk
Mih donkey eat with a knife and fork

By the time they had gotten to the fourth or fifth round of the song, the melody had spread through the crowd and even Dru had joined in. At a sharp slope, Bouki stopped. He turned in every direction as if he was lost and looking for the way. The song tapered off, ending with a little boy on his father's shoulders who giggled as he sang the last lines.

Mih donkey eat, mih donkey sleep
Mih donkey kick with his two hind feet

The crowd grew silent when Bouki turned to them.

"It gets harder from here," he called out. "We're going to have to walk single file the rest of the way." He jerked his head at a young boy near him, who looked about the same age as Malik. "You're going to have to help the smaller ones." The boy nodded, as did all the other little kids who thought they were old enough to help. Even Maya stood up straighter and grabbed the hand of a child who could only have been her younger sister. The two of them had the same pattern of cornrows braided into their hair with a cluster of white beads at the end of each plait.

Wind whistled out of the narrow spaces between the stones. Lightning flashed in the sky again, and Corinne squinted, hoping to make out the figure in the clouds again, but also hoping that she didn't see anything.

"Hurry," Bouki said.

He directed two men ahead of everyone, then took a small boy against his hip as he continued up. The path was nearly vertical in some places, making it necessary to move with hands and feet. On narrow paths, smaller children were passed up to waiting hands. The going was much slower, and they were all drenched to the skin. The men stopped near a large stone and called back something Corinne couldn't make out. Bouki put down the child he was holding and disappeared behind the stone. Moments later, a large branch went tumbling down the side of the mountain, and Bouki waved everyone on.

They had to stop more frequently to clear the path. The crowd, soaked to the skin, shivering, and tense, grumbled. Several children cried and the rain came down harder. Corinne wondered how long it would be until they reached the caves.

Thunder exploded across the sky and something above them cracked. The ground shook. A moment later, a large boulder tumbled down the hill.

"Back!" Bouki called.

The rock splintered as it descended, coming fast. It bounced off a ledge just above them, spitting rocks and clumps of dirt onto the crowd before continuing down the mountain. The ground shuddered once again, then became still.

Bouki led them forward again, but another tumble of wet rocks fell, hitting him and knocking him off his feet as they tumbled after the first boulder. Malik ran to help. A gash at Bouki's shoulder bled. He put a hand over it, and someone from the crowd ripped a sleeve off their shirt to bandage the cut. Hugo pushed through to the boys and picked up Bouki off the ground as easily as if he was a baby.

"I'm okay," Bouki protested.

Hugo set him down but watched carefully.

Bouki continued on, but warned everyone to stay as close to the side as possible. They squeezed together on a narrow ledge, pressing their bodies into the mountain.

"Get away! Get off me!" Maya's mother screamed. She lurched forward, nearly knocking someone off the path. She looked terrified as she held on to a baby, and Maya and her younger siblings cowered around their mother's legs.

"What is it?" Pierre asked.

The woman narrowed her eyes and jutted her lips at a small hunched woman with her gray hair braided in cornrows. She looked almost as old as the white witch. "Her skin is fire!" said Maya's mother. "Feel it!"

Someone reached out to the woman, and the word *jumbie* rippled through the crowd. As people turned to look at those around them, several pairs of eyes settled on Corinne. She felt their gazes against her skin like insects boring into rotting wood.

"Wasn't it a jumbie who saved your children?" Mrs. Rootsingh asked above the grumbling voices.

Corinne moved to the old woman and took her by the elbow. She almost pulled back because it was true that the woman's skin was fire hot, but she didn't want to give anyone the satisfaction. Pierre gave her a questioning look and she shook her head very slightly to let him know that she was fine. The rain drove harder, but no one moved.

Allan went to Corinne and held the old woman's other hand. "I was a jumbie, too," he said. "And Corinne saved me."

Mrs. Ramdeen looked at her boy adoringly. She tugged at the fabric of her sari where the rain had plastered it to her legs and walked over to help the old woman along. Mrs. Ramdeen's eyes flicked to Corinne a moment, but like Corinne and Allan, she didn't let go. Together, they walked on.

"Anybody who doesn't want to be around a jumbie can head back down the mountain," Bouki said loudly. "The rest of us—"

Lightning and thunder simultaneously ripped across the sky. Every drop of rain illuminated in the light, and every creased worry line and every tensed muscle in the crowd was thrown into sharp relief. Once again the ground rumbled, stronger this time than the last.

Bouki's eyes became wide. Malik immediately began to shove people up ahead, to where there was an overhang in the rocks. Corinne and Dru followed his lead, pushing and pulling as many forward on the narrow strip cut into the mountain as quickly as they could manage.

"Dru!" Mrs. Rootsingh called.

"I'm coming, Mama!" Dru said, but she wasn't. She was handing a small boy to his mother.

The ground again shook violently and the sound of tumbling rocks grew louder overhead.

As the last of the crowd made it across the path, a river of mud came sliding down the mountain, bringing rocks and bushes and a few smaller trees with it. The mud caught Corinne's feet, but she managed to get her arms around a medium-sized tree in the path of the mudslide. Others were not so lucky. People got overtaken by the mud, knocked off their feet and pulled down the mountain. Anyone close enough reached their hands out, grabbing what they could—arms, legs, or bits of clothing to pull the fallen to safety. The mudslide grew wider as it came. Plants and rocks peeked out through the rolling earth, and then got sucked under. The silver belly of a dead fish flashed at the surface one moment and disappeared the next. A matted, broken wing floated by. Bouki shoved Malik and Dru out of the way, putting them on one side of the river of mud and debris. Corinne was still holding on to the tree as the muck spread around her, too wide for her to grab Bouki's outstretched arm. Pierre reached from the other side, but the mud widened further, pushing him away, too.

"Corinne! You're going to have to jump," Bouki said.

The little tree started to bend from Corinne's weight and the force of the mud pushing against it. Corinne wrapped her feet around the strained trunk, and it bowed further. Corinne's hands were wet and her grip was slipping. If she didn't fall soon, the tree trunk would break and take her tumbling down with it. Either would send her into the river of mud, and straight down the mountain over sharp rocks and steep cliffs.

"I'll catch you," Pierre shouted. "Jump!" He reached toward Corinne, still being pushed back by the widening mud river. Corinne knew he wouldn't let her fall. On Pierre's side were most of the crowd and the safety of the caves. On the other were all of her friends. The trunk creaked and began to crack. It was now or never.

Corinne tucked her feet under her the way she did when she was jumping from one coconut tree to another. She leapt off, landing against Bouki on one side of the river. On the other side, Pierre let his arms go limp at his sides. His body crumpled with the same worry Corinne had learned to recognize in his face.

When the mud stopped running, Bouki tested his feet on it, but it was still unsteady and slick. "We can't cross it," he said.

"What now?" Dru asked. She looked at her family on the other side of the mud.

Malik pointed in a different direction.

"We will have to go around," Bouki said. He looked across at Hugo and Pierre. "Don't worry, I know another way. Get inside."

Everyone but Mr. and Mrs. Rootsingh, Pierre, and Hugo made for the caves.

"I will be okay, Mama," Dru shouted.

"We'll be there soon," Bouki added.

Corinne couldn't think of what to say.

Their parents stood in the rain watching until Bouki led them up another path and out of sight.

10

The Weight of Water

The roof of the white witch's house was gone. The wind had ripped it right off from over her head and had peeled the wood from the walls like skin from a fig. The witch had no choice but to cower under the only solid thing in that house—the long wooden table—and wait while the water poured in around her from the sky, and from the rising swamp.

She knew very well that one hurricane didn't follow another on the same path so quickly. It meant that something was amiss. She scratched at the bare spots on her head as she considered what exactly was the problem. A bright red ibis feather floated past her on the

< 66 >

swamp, pummeled by the rain, and a thought suddenly hit her.

She peered into the storm, telling it, "Oh. I see."

After the first storm, the white witch's house, which had stood on a small, muddy island in the swamp for ages and ages, had been reduced to little more than a few jagged sticks jutting up to the sky.

Most of the seeds and leaves she collected for medicines had spilled onto the sodden floor of the shack. Their carefully wrapped papers were torn and soaked, the bags ripped, and a few bottles lay cracked on the floor.

Things like this were not a bother. There were always ingredients that could be gathered. Though some were more difficult to procure than others and it would take time to reassemble her stores, the witch had been in this position before. Many times, in fact. Every hurricane season she braced for the worst, and survived, usually needing to climb her old bones up to fix the galvanized roof or nail more wood into the rickety walls. She had always managed. But this time, she would need a new shelter. The swamp provided privacy, but not much else.

The water rose higher, lifting the legs of her wooden table and making it wobble. It was time to go. The witch scraped together what was left of her patience. Her body was stiff and cold, and moving was excruciating, but there was no choice now. With her oil lamp, some matches, and a small bag of herbs, the white witch moved down the slick stone path that led away from her house, taking uneven steps as she navigated across. Without even looking at her feet, she knew the exact places to step that would not make her slip and fall. It was, after all, a path of her own invention, designed to keep people out, to force them into the foul-smelling swamp water, to make them think twice before coming to her door. It had not always worked. She would never say so out loud, but in truth, she was the tiniest bit grateful for that.

The witch made it to a network of mangrove trees where the roots rose out of the water, their thick trunks arcing high overhead like a natural roof. The roots twisted together tightly enough to make sturdy, if breezy, walls. It would be a safe harbor provided the witch could find a deep-enough space in which to settle herself. With the brackish water up to her knees, the witch followed the trees, looking for anywhere she could rest easily and wait out this next storm. As she moved, the water deepened, lapping up to her thighs, and then all the way to her waist before she spotted a good place. But to get there, she would have to swim.

For anyone else, this would mean the end of the meager supplies they had brought along. But not for the white witch. She untied a cloth at her waist and wrung out the water. Then she put the herbs and the lamp on her head, covering it with the cloth and wrapping the ends under her chin before tying it securely. She eased into the swamp, keeping her head above the surface, and made for the little alcove. The weight of the water in her skirts and blouse made things more difficult, but the witch understood how panic could undo even the best plans. She moved slowly, stopping to float a little and breathe, then continued on until she was close enough to the little root cavern.

Once there, she made a final push and grabbed on. She looped her fingers into some of the higher roots and pulled herself inside with her one good arm. The useless arm made a good-enough prop when she needed to rest, but it could do little else.

With patience and after several slips of her hand, she got most of her body into the shelter. She settled her rump against a thick root, unwrapped the cloth, and took down the lamp, matches, and herbs. She pushed them into a space above her head for safekeeping. Then she pulled her legs in.

"Look at me, folded up and jammed in this hole like a rabbit." She laughed, and her laugh turned into a cough. "What a way to spend a day."

The hurricane blew louder and the rain came down harder.

The witch moved as far back into the little space as she could, then settled against the mangrove roots, trying to ignore the way they dug into her back and sides. She closed her eyes. It would be a long time before she could get out and back to her house to fix it. Maybe it was the roots poking at her, or the wet sticky feeling of her clothes against her body, or the fact that she knew for certain she would get no rest in this space, but the witch called out in irritation, "Water jumbies on land. Land jumbies in the water. I suppose there's only the sky left to bawl."

As soon as she said it, her jaw slackened. The witch remembered a storm from years ago, eerily similar to the one that raged all around her now. She looked at the gray sheets of rain as if she was looking out at the long-lost face of a friend. "Well," she said. "You come back again? But what for this time?"

She sighed. She was old old old, too old for all of it. She wished to sleep. It had been years since she had had a good sleep. She was always up at midnight to catch the best of the magic from the herbs and plants she picked. She could not sleep past the first crack of dawn because the scarlet ibises that were her neighbors were a flapping, squawking riot in the morning as they set out. She often slept in the afternoon after market, when the sun was hottest, but even then, it was not enough sleep. Never enough. She was tired.

So tired.

There was nothing to do now but wait. She wondered how long the rain would last this time. The water in the swamp rose higher. It wet the hem of her skirt. Then it covered her hips. Its cold on her old bones made her even more uncomfortable. Then the water was to her waist. Then it almost covered all of her bad arm.

The witch watched the water's surface ripple under the weight of the raindrops as it rose and rose. She watched it cover the trunk of the largest tree in the swamp, which housed the majority of her bright, noisy neighbors.

"You won't hear me complain again!" she said to the tree, since none of the birds were present.

She thought of all the things she still needed to tell the girl, the half-jumbie like herself. "She isn't too stupid," the witch thought aloud. "She will figure it out."

By the time the water had begun to soak into the short white braids at the back of her head, the witch was perfectly certain Corinne would be fine.

When the water touched the bristly hair of her chin, her eyes brightened. She remembered Corinne looking out on the horizon.

"Oh, I see now," she said. "She wasn't looking up high enough."

The water was up to her bottom lip. As it continued to rise, the white witch sent a final message. It rippled out on the water, stretching out of the swamp and into the sea.

"I hope you know you can't fix this mess alone."

And then the witch slept.

11

Adrift

In the churning sea, Mama D'Leau's body whipped through the sand-filled water. She could barely see or feel the currents to find her way. She had a vague sense of the coral reef to her left, but where it was exactly, and how far, she couldn't say. She hated being turned this way, like food stirred in a pot for someone's dinner.

She tried to pull herself together. In all her born days she had never been treated so.

You rule the water, you will let a little rain stop you? she asked herself.

She strained against the pull of the currents, twisting her body to pry herself from their grip. But nothing worked. She was as helpless as a piece of driftwood, or a broken sprig of sargassum.

The current turned, and her tail screwed up and around her body. She nearly squeezed herself to death. Then the current released and bashed Mama D'Leau against the surface of a rock. She felt a sharp edge slice her skin. Her thick braided hair provided some cushion, but she hit her head so hard she could barely think.

The strength of the storm struck fear into her heart.

The water pulled her away and crashed her into the rocks again. She felt the sting of another cut near the end of her tail. The pain traveled up her body and brought tears to her eyes that mixed with the saltwater of the sea. She wrapped her tail around the rock, anchoring herself in place. She would have to wait out the storm there, cowering, angry that it made her feel so small and helpless.

As she pressed into the side of the rock and felt the sea beating around her, trying to pry her loose so it could bash her again, she heard the words of the witch coming to her like an arrow through the chaos of the stormy sea.

I know, Mama D'Leau replied. *I know.*

She waited for the white witch to respond, to make a suggestion, to say something typically cold and harsh, but there was no answer.

12

Back at Last

Bouki led them through the cracks of the mountain, searching for another path. The wind whipped branches past them and sent mud and stone hurtling toward their bodies. It was almost impossible to hear, so Bouki led them with hand gestures, beckoning when it was safe, holding up his palm when it wasn't. A gust blew Malik off the path. Corinne grabbed his hand quickly, but a bird slammed into her wrist. Her grip slackened as the bird fell limp to the rocks below, and Malik slipped from her grasp. Bouki caught Malik's other hand just in time. Corinne and Dru grabbed hold and together they pulled him back up.

"We should go back," Corinne shouted into the rain.

"We can't." Bouki pointed his dripping chin in the direction they had come. Another mudslide had closed off the path behind them. The only way was forward.

Malik pushed himself into a little cleft between two large rocks. He leaned there, panting for a moment, then shifted his weight to get out and slipped into the shadows in the blink of an eye.

"Malik!" Bouki screamed his brother's name, though Corinne couldn't hear it. Another gust blew across them, whipping the name from his mouth, and leaving only his open mouth and strained face for Corinne and Dru to read. He rushed after his brother, holding on to the two sides of the rocks and peering into the darkness.

"Where is he?" Corinne shouted over the roar of the storm.

Dru pushed past the two of them and looked in. "Here!" she said. Then she slipped between the rocks and disappeared.

Corinne and Bouki looked in. They couldn't see anything.

"Come!" Dru called.

"Do you see a way in?" Corinne asked Bouki.

"No. There's nothing."

Corinne wedged herself into the crevice between the rocks and tried to push through. The rocks scraped against her arms and chest, but a moment later, she was on the other side, in a dark space with Dru and Malik standing next to her. Bouki was still looking in, squinting. "You're going to have to squeeze through," she said.

Bouki looked skeptical, but he sucked in his stomach and entered the sliver sideways, keeping his face flat. Corinne, Dru, and Malik grabbed his arm and pulled. Bouki fell on the rocky floor of the little cave and looked up at his brother. "Hello," he said.

Malik pointed at the space around them. Bouki turned.

It looked like any other cave at first, but as Corinne's eyes adjusted to the low light, she saw drawings on the walls in red mud and black and white clay. The entire cave was filled with them. There were pictures of people walking, planting, and hunting the small animals of the island.

"Is that an agouti?" Dru asked.

"If it is, it's the biggest one I've ever seen," Corinne said. "And there's a caiman here." She pointed at a painting of a long, low creature with a man standing near it, about to thrust a spear into its body.

Malik pulled Bouki to his feet and brought him to another part of the cave. Jumping, he jabbed his finger at one of the drawings. It didn't look like the others. Like a child's scrawl in the sand, it was a big round head with three other heads circling it. Each had two dots inside them, like eyes, only the eyes were lopsided and smeared.

"I remember this," Bouki said.

"How?" Corinne asked.

"We've been here before."

"When?" Dru asked. "Malik found it by accident."

Bouki's eyes glazed as if he was seeing a memory play out in the dark cave.

"What is this place?" Corinne asked.

"We played here," Bouki said. "When we were little."

Corinne looked at small Malik, wondering how long ago that was and how much littler he could have been then. "When you were on your own?" she asked.

Bouki squeezed his eyes shut. His shoulders slumped, and his forehead knitted.

Malik walked around the cave, touching the walls lightly with his fingertips. Corinne could usually read him, but right now she couldn't tell what he was thinking at all.

When Bouki opened his eyes again, they were watery and red. "We weren't alone," he said. "Not then."

"Who was with you?" Dru asked.

Bouki shook his head and sniffled, then pushed his shoulders back. "We can't stay here," he said loudly. "We have to find a way out." He looked to Malik, who was beckoning them with one hand as he looked at another spot on the cave wall.

They went to him and found another drawing with four circles, this time two on the top and two on the bottom. The top ones had dot eyes and the bottom ones were empty.

Bouki took his brother's hand a little roughly and pulled him. "This way," he said.

"How are you so sure of the way?" Dru asked.

Corinne caught Dru's eye and shook her head just enough that Dru alone would see it.

Dru bit her lip and followed in silence.

Bouki led them through a series of dark passageways. He moved quickly, as if he knew the space by heart. Malik continued to trace his fingers against the walls, but he did not remove his other hand from his brother's. Corinne and Dru sometimes had to run to keep up with the boys. Every now and then they would look at each other. Corinne read worry in Dru's face, and she wondered if Dru saw the same in hers.

After a few minutes, the path widened and light filtered from above. The sound of the howling rain seemed distant, but the thunder continued to rage, sending shivers through the mountain that loosened dust and an occasional rock. It was like being in the belly of a monster just waking up. Dru and Corinne squeezed closer together every time a new rumble shook another bit of the mountain loose around them.

They turned a corner to a cave that opened like a mouth to the outside. Bouki let go of Malik's hand and held up his palm. Everyone stopped and waited. He moved to the opening and looked out, then came back to them, wet and dripping. He shook his head and led them back to the path.

Farther up there was a fork. One way led down, and

the other up. Bouki moved toward the right path, which led down, but Malik grabbed him and pointed to the left.

"I don't think so, brother," Bouki said.

But Malik refused to go to the right. He stood rigid at the entrance to the left path, with his arms folded and his eyes pleading.

"What would it hurt to go this way?" Corinne asked. "We can always double back if we need to."

Bouki took a deep, jagged breath and followed his brother.

"What if we get lost in here?" Dru whispered. "What if we spend the rest of our lives wandering around a dark, damp cave filled with muddy drawings?"

"That's not going to happen," Corinne said.

"How do you know?"

Corinne whispered, "Because I think they know exactly where they are."

The path rose steeply, so they had to use their hands for balance as they scrambled up. Pressure built in Corinne's ears and her head felt like it was filled with cotton. She swallowed hard until her ears popped. As they kept climbing, it happened over and over again. Every time, she had to stop to clear her head.

Gradually the air became cooler and less damp. Corinne felt glad for the comfort, but she also knew that with every step she was much farther from her papa. He would never be able to find her now.

"Where are we?" she asked. "How long until we reach . . . wherever you're taking us?" There was no response from the boys.

The path leveled off and opened up to a large cave. The light was still dim outside, but the rain wasn't falling as hard as before. The children ventured to the mouth of the cave and looked out. The whole island was laid out beneath them in muted green behind a haze of gray clouds and sheets of rain.

"Are we in the clouds?" Dru asked.

Malik smiled and nodded.

Corinne scanned the sky for the face she had seen earlier. She still wondered if it had been a trick of her mind, despite the boys' stories of the god Huracan. Surely gods didn't show themselves.

"We're nearly there," Bouki announced.

"Where?" Dru asked.

Bouki pointed to a path that led away from the cave up a series of stone steps.

"What about mudslides?" Corinne asked, peering over the lip of the cave to the sharp drop that led to the bottom of the mountain.

"The path is clear," he said. "Come on." His voice was small and tight. Whatever was at the top of those stairs made him nervous.

Corinne's heart beat hard against the bones of her

chest. She hesitated, but knew that there was no choice but to keep going.

Bouki led them up. Near the top, he paused, stood on one foot, then hopped over one step before continuing. Behind him, Malik did the same thing, then turned back to grin at the girls.

"Careful of that one," Bouki said. "It's a little rickety."

Dru and Corinne shared a confused look, and Corinne folded her lips between her teeth. They moved forward, avoiding the stair as instructed.

At the top, there was a smooth, winding path of rocks. The mist was so thick that it was difficult to see what lay beyond it. Corinne felt its chill settle on her skin, closing in as if something large and formless had dropped a cloak around her. She wanted to get off the mountain, but she didn't know the way back down.

Malik moved forward and disappeared into the soft gray mist with Bouki right behind him. But while Malik skipped ahead, Bouki's steps were slower and his body sagged, as if moving forward was an effort. Corinne wondered if he was feeling the chill too, or if it was something else entirely. She went to Bouki's side. Dru took the other side and together they followed Malik into the cold cloud.

They kept walking until the mist cleared and they could see a wide plateau at the end of the path. Beyond that was a single large doorway cut into the face of the mountain.

Bouki stopped, and he, Dru, and Corinne waited as if they expected something to come out of the doorway any moment. Only Malik and the clouds continued to move. Wisps of gray and white slipped around each other until Corinne was sure she saw a face, but a moment later the wisps had changed into nothing at all. The clouds continued shifting around her, teasing her with nearly formed faces that quickly turned into other shapes. Their mist traced Corinne's skin and raised her pores.

Bouki moved forward, walking through a patch of grass in front of the door. His breathing was deep, but uneven, as if he couldn't quite catch his breath.

When they reached the middle of the grassy area, a woman stepped out of the dark arch. She was wide, wearing a long dress of red patterned cloth that wrapped around her chest and a colorful head tie done up with a twist around the crown. She wiped her hands with a towel. Her bare feet slapped the stones outside the doorway and mashed the low grass as she walked toward them.

With one hand, Corinne grasped at her neck, searching for her mama's necklace, as she reached for Dru's fingers with the other.

"Don't be frightened," the woman said. She paused, still a little distance away, and cocked her head, studying Bouki and Malik. In a moment, her pleasant, welcoming face crumpled and her bottom lip quivered. "Oh, *mes petits*," she said to the boys. "You've come back at last."

13

Dodo Piti Popo

"Look, everyone! Come and see!" the woman called out.

A few faces peered from the shadows of the mountain doorway. Each of them was the same reddish brown as the boys' own faces. Some were topped with the same corkscrew-curly hair, and others had hair as pin straight as Dru's. All of them had wide smiles and dark eyes. They looked like a family.

"Look at you! So big now." The woman walked slowly toward the boys, as if they were a pair of wild animals that might try to run. She kept her eyes on them, and her hands at her sides. Malik pushed his shoulders back and waited, unmoving as she approached, but Bouki pulled him back, placing his own body like a shield between his brother and the woman.

She stopped. "You are Bouki and Malik, not so?"

Malik peeked around Bouki.

"We know what our names are," Bouki said.

"How do *you* know what their names are?" Dru asked.

"They are ours," the woman said. She took another small step toward Bouki. "I'm your aunty Lu."

Bouki shook his head. "We don't know you."

Malik turned a frown on his brother.

"We don't," Bouki said to Malik.

"Don't worry," Aunty Lu said. "We are just surprised and happy to see you."

A few more people moved out onto the plateau. The women wore bright patterned dresses with their hair in a single thick plait wrapped around their heads or long down their backs. Some had shawls draped over their shoulders. The men wore long pants and embroidered shirts. All of them had skin that gleamed bronze, as if they were lit by the early rays of sunset.

The warmth of this smiling, silent group of people drove the chill from Corinne's body.

"You are Ava and Diego's sons," Aunty Lu said, wiping tears from her eyes. More people crowded in behind her. "And you have been gone a very, very long time."

"Come," she went on. "The rain will thicken again soon, and this is no place to be in a storm."

"It doesn't look like it was too bad up here," Corinne said.

"It rarely is," Aunty Lu said, pointing toward the stone doorway. "But yesterday a storm, today a storm, who knows what is really going on?" A bolt of lightning lit up her face as she stared out. Her body stiffened at the flash. She got behind the four of them and pushed them gently toward the great stone door. "Quickly!"

The mountain arch led to a short passageway. On the other side was a small village of round, thatched-roof structures. The wooden houses were clustered together, connected with a network of hammocks. Nestled among them were banana trees. To one side was a neatly planted area of vegetables and herbs about the same size as the land the houses occupied. Tall stalks of corn waved over smaller plants like pak choi and bodi. The mountain surrounded the village like a pair of cupped hands.

Aunty Lu led the children to a large central building. Like the others, it was round. It had windows in each wall panel, and four doors, one in each cardinal direction. Inside, the contents of a huge black pot boiled on the fire. The scent made Corinne's stomach growl. The woman stirring the pot watched curiously with a slightly furrowed forehead.

"I'm sure you must be hungry," Aunty Lu said. "It's a

long way from the valley." She ushered them to a low table with benches near the woman who was cooking. The pot was filled with vegetables: potatoes, carrots, yams, pumpkin. A dasheen bush lay on a table behind Aunty Lu, along with the rinds of squeezed lemons and the remnants of a few chopped herbs. A salty, earthy scent rose up into the air.

The heat of the fire gave Corinne immediate relief from the cold. Malik stuck his feet out as close to the fire as he could and wriggled his toes. Corinne and Dru kicked off their sandals and followed suit. In moments they would be warm and dry.

Malik looked perfectly comfortable, but Bouki sat at the very edge of the bench, ready to spring up any moment.

Aunty Lu moved over to the woman at the pot. They leaned their heads together talking.

"Do you think she is telling the truth?" Corinne asked.

Bouki shrugged. His fists were tight on his legs as if he was holding on to something that was precious and slippery.

"Do you remember Ava and Diego?" Corinne asked again.

Malik shrugged.

"You resemble them," Dru said. "Maybe they really are your family."

"Then where have they been all this time?" Bouki hissed.

Aunty Lu came to them with a platter that held four

neatly folded dark green leaves with something steaming inside each one. They smelled spicy and meaty. Aunty Lu put the platter on the table and smiled. "Eat."

Malik dug in immediately, untying the vine around his bundle, then unfolding the leaf carefully. A puff of steam rose from it and flavored the air with peppers, raisins, and beef. Inside the leaf was a lump of yellow dough that looked about to burst open with food. Corinne's stomach growled again, more loudly this time, and all eyes turned to her.

"*Pastelles*," Aunty Lu explained. She rested a hand on Corinne's shoulder. "Eat before this one swallows up the rest of you!"

Malik was already biting into his own pastelle as Corinne and Dru were unwrapping theirs. As soon as she bit in, Corinne's mouth watered even more. The yellow corn-flour dough on the outside melted on her tongue while the ground meat filling danced flavor around her mouth.

Malik gave Aunty Lu a slight nod of thanks as he polished off his pastelle. Bouki had not moved. His pastelle remained on the platter, steaming. Aunty Lu uncovered a bowl of water and approached Bouki with it and a fresh piece of white linen. She touched his shoulder gently where he had been cut by the rock. Bouki leaned slightly away, but didn't flinch. She carefully untied the piece of shirt that had bound the wound, and used the water to clean it off. Then she rewrapped it with the linen.

"Thanks," he said gruffly.

Aunty Lu smiled and backed away slowly, as if she was still afraid he might bolt.

Corinne looked at Bouki's uneaten pastelle. "If you're not going to eat it . . ." she said, making a big show of reaching for it.

"You can have it if you want. I'm not hungry." Bouki turned away.

"It's not me you're hurting if you don't eat," Aunty Lu said. She placed cups in front of each of them, and poured steaming milk from a small pitcher.

Malik reached for his cup immediately and nearly dropped it.

"Sorry, baby, it's still too hot. But I will cool it for you." Aunty Lu took Malik's milk and poured it into another cup, then again into the first one, going back and forth. Her hands seesawed in the air, and the milk made long, splashing arcs. She handed one of the cups back to Malik, who downed the milk in almost one gulp.

"You always did like to cool your milk a little before you drank it, *petit*," she said quietly. Aunty Lu cooled all of the milk the same way, handing off each one. She left Bouki for last. He sat stiffly, looking out the window at the clouds knotting and unknotting around the village. In every lightning flash a new picture formed, always moving, always different, like a series of faces observing them from every angle.

Dru leaned close to Bouki. "The storm is getting bad again. How safe are the caves?"

"Everyone will be fine," Bouki said.

"Who is in the caves?" Aunty Lu asked.

"Our families," Corinne said. She swallowed hard, remembering the look on her papa's face when she jumped away from him. "When the storm started, Bouki and Malik led everyone to the mountains for safety."

Aunty Lu beamed. "What brave, smart boys!" She clapped Malik on the back, nodding vigorously. "They were right to lead people here. They will be safe until the storm passes.

"You will be safe here in the village, too," she said, looking from Corinne to Dru. "There is no way back down tonight, you hear me?"

Dru bit her lip, and Corinne nodded.

Corinne cleared her throat. "You said that this wasn't a regular storm . . . Aunty . . . Lu," she began. "Bouki told us about a god—"

"Huracan," Aunty Lu finished. "You remember that story?" She turned a great smile on the boys. Malik beamed back, but Bouki scowled and looked away. "Yes. Huracan controls the storms. Even the air and the sea answer when he cries out."

Corinne thought about Mama D'Leau in the water and understood the jumbie's fear now.

"Why is he here now?" Corinne asked.

Aunty Lu raised an eyebrow. "Who could say? We can only hope that whatever it is that made him this angry will get fixed soon, and we will all survive until it does."

A cold, wet wind blew the frayed edges of the thatched roofs like strands of hair.

Corinne shivered. She wondered how everyone was making out in the caves below. Did they have blankets? Could they make fire? Was there enough to drink?

"You look tired," Aunty Lu said. "Come." She led them through the rain to a nearby house.

Inside smelled of sweet wood, cocoa, and fresh linens. Corinne was grateful for the dry and warmth, but she worried about her papa. When he didn't see them come back like they had promised, he wouldn't be able to rest.

Aunty Lu wrapped them in towels and pulled out linens from a carved wood wardrobe.

Corinne's muscles ached. She helped spread the sheets and blankets on rolled mattresses and cushions on the floor, side by side with the others making up their beds for the night.

In a moment when Aunty Lu was close to Corinne's ear, she whispered, "He doesn't talk much, does he?"

"Malik?" Corinne whispered back. "You have to know how to listen."

She nodded, but tears welled in her eyes. "They were gone so long. Who took care of them?"

"They took care of each other," Corinne said.

Aunty Lu clasped her hands at her heart. "They were alone? They were just babies. It's no wonder he doesn't talk." She jutted her mouth toward Malik and clucked her tongue.

"They weren't always alone," Corinne said. At a glance from Aunty Lu, she stiffened. "I mean, they had each other, and Dru, and me." Hugo was a story for the boys to tell themselves.

"Oh, of course," Aunty Lu said. "I meant, maybe losing his parents, and being separated from all of us . . ."

"What happened to them? Ava and Diego?" Corinne asked.

Aunty Lu closed her eyes for a moment and sighed deeply. "They took the boys down the mountain for supplies. It was Malik's first time. Bouki had gone dozens of times before. It was always the same: a quick trip down to the markets and back home in two, three days. But then it was four days, then five." Aunty Lu's breath rattled as if something was stuck in her chest. "When they didn't return after a week, we went to search for them. We found Ava first, near the base of the mountain. And then Diego. Both had large stones in their hands as if they were trying to fend something off. They had been attacked by an animal. The boys were gone. We thought they had been carried off."

Corinne's throat burned. "Shouldn't you have checked?

Couldn't you have looked better?" Her voice cracked and she was near tears.

Aunty Lu embraced her in a pair of thick, warm arms. "We searched everywhere we could. Down in the market, and all the way out to the sea. We asked everyone, but no one had seen two little boys."

Corinne wiped her face in her shirt.

"We gave up." Aunty Lu glanced at the boys. "We shouldn't have."

Corinne wanted to know how long they looked and how far before they gave up. What was the exact measurement of time and space before someone stopped looking? But Aunty Lu changed her tone.

"And you? Where is your family?"

"My papa is in the caves with everyone else."

"Oh, love," Aunty Lu said, holding Corinne again. "You will see your papa soon."

Aunty Lu hummed and moved to say goodnight to Bouki and Malik. Two smaller children, a boy and girl, came bounding in from the rain and peered around the doorway.

"You've come to see your cousins?" Aunty Lu asked.

Bouki and Malik looked up.

"Your father's family," Aunty Lu explained, gesturing to the little boy and girl. "Though here, everybody is some kind of pumpkin-vine relation."

The children grinned eagerly.

"So am I making up beds for the two of you as well?"

They nodded again and filed inside, sitting next to Malik with wonder.

Aunty Lu got out more linens. She continued to hum, and her tune rose and fell with the wind outside. The two little children took up the pieces of the song and added words.

Dodo piti popo
Piti popo pa vle dodo . . .

Malik tilted his head and giggled, then sang along.

Zambi a ke mange le
Sukugnan ke suce san.

Aunty Lu paused when Malik joined in. Then she began to sing the words, too, as she whipped the sheets out into the air and smoothed them with the palm of her hand.

"How does Malik know this song?" Dru whispered to Corinne.

As a reply Corinne pointed to Bouki, whose face had stilled. He seemed dazed and lulled. He looked nothing like the Bouki Corinne knew.

"What are they singing?" Dru asked him.

"It's a lullaby," he said.

"Sukugnan ke suce san!" Malik sang with Aunty Lu and the two cousins. Malik bared his teeth at them, making them scream and collapse into giggles on the floor.

"What does it mean?" Corinne asked.

"It's about a baby being eaten by a jumbie," Bouki said.

"You can understand the language?" Dru asked. "I've never heard it before."

"It's patois," Bouki said. "My parents spoke it." As the song started up again, Bouki translated.

Sleep little baby
The little baby doesn't want to sleep
The jumbie will eat him
The soucouyant will suck his blood!

Dru squeezed Corinne's hand, tightening her grip with every line. Malik and his cousins had settled into a pantomime, with the little ones waiting for Malik to show his teeth and attack.

"This is a terrible lullaby," Dru whispered to Corinne.

"It's just a song, Dru." Corinne looked at Aunty Lu. She seemed so nice and helpful. She had greeted them and fed them, and was now making up beds for them. The storm whipped up on the other side of the mountain, but all the danger seemed far away up here on the plateau. Only a thick, soaking rain and a song about children being eaten up troubled them here. Corinne thought about the old woman on the way up with skin as hot as fire, and how she had frightened everyone around her without doing anything at all. Corinne had defended her then, knowing there was nothing to fear. But did she really know? Jumbies were feared for a reason. There was a reason no one ever went into the woods after sunset. There was a reason people walked backwards into their houses late at night. It was so jumbies wouldn't follow them. Because that was what jumbies did. They tricked people and then killed them.

As she watched Aunty Lu tuck everyone into the made-up beds, Corinne wondered who this woman was really. She had been deceived by a sweet-looking woman before. Corinne's hand fluttered down to her thigh where a long, thin scar, winding like a rivulet, cut into the brown of her skin. This had been her reward for letting her guard down because she didn't see the danger behind a lovely smile.

She needed to think, but the song, the steaming pastelle, the warm milk, and the fresh, crisp sheets made her sleepy. She would close her eyes just for a moment, then she would think of a way to find out just who Aunty Lu was. Corinne was not going to be deceived twice.

14

Into the Fire

A crack of thunder woke Corinne. It was still pitch-black outside, and for a few moments, she had no idea where she was or how long she had slept. Her surroundings came to her in degrees: first the soft layer of cushions she was sleeping on, then the gentle breathing of her friends, then the dark outline of Aunty Lu's house. She listened to the sound of rain pounding the roof, the walls, and the soft ground outside.

Corinne propped herself up on her elbows as she tried to remember everything that had happened the day before. Then across the village, she saw the glow of light deep inside the mountain. It pulsed like a heartbeat. Corinne could almost feel its warmth, even though it was far away and separated by a field of rain. She felt desperate to get closer. She rose up out of her bed, and the sheets that covered her fell away. She knew she would be soaked walking across the grass, but she didn't care. That fire would warm and dry her.

The warmth from the light penetrated her chest and radiated outward until it reached her fingers, her toes, the top of her head. She was going to it, rain or not.

Standing, Corinne slipped on the smooth, wet wood of the bedroom. Rain must have blown in through the open doorway. She resumed walking more carefully, taking the time to plant one foot solidly on the floor before lifting the other. She reached the doorway and felt the rain against her body. There was a sizzling sound that she couldn't quite place. For a moment she thought it was the firelight calling her, but that was ridiculous.

Corinne barely felt either the mud and wet grass beneath her feet or her clothes heavy and soaked with rain. She was too focused on reaching the fire and . . . touching it.

At the entrance to the passageway cut into the mountain, Corinne spotted someone hunched near the fire. The flames painted the old man bright yellow and orange. Each of his wrinkles made deep striping shadows on his cheeks and forehead. His body was wrapped in a blanket, his long black hair neatly tied at his neck. The old man looked up at Corinne, tilted his head, then looked into the fire again.

"I didn't mean to disturb you," she said.

"You aren't," the old man said.

"The fire looked so . . . inviting."

"Fire calls fire." Every word the old man said was slow and careful.

"Who are you?"

"I am the cacique. The elder of the village. I care for everyone here."

"Do you know my friends Bouki and Malik?"

"I know them, their parents, their family."

"So they are from here," Corinne said.

The cacique nodded. "It is good to have them back."

The rain fell harder, in thick torrents that cut them off completely from the rest of the village.

"And you?" he asked. "Who are you?"

"Corinne La Mer. I live by the sea."

"I can smell the sea on you," he said. "And the land too. And . . ."

"What?" Corinne asked.

"Fire."

Corinne knew the smell of fire, the earthy and sharp scent of burning wood, the fresh smell of herbs crisping at the bottom of a pot. Fire brought out the essence of everything, until it consumed it completely. But all Corinne could smell right then was the flat, choking scent of ash.

"Do you need help getting back inside?" Corinne asked. "You must be uncomfortable sitting on the stones like that. I can walk you back to your house."

"I'm watching the storm," the cacique said. "This is a good place to do that."

"Why?" Corinne asked. "There is nothing you can do."

"When gods speak we must listen carefully." He pulled the blanket closer around his shoulders. "Without putting our own selves in the way."

"You're listening to Huracan?"

"So you know? Huracan summons the wind and rain and wields lightning like a sword. He twirls it in his fingers and jabs it at his mark. He doesn't miss and he never falters. He will destroy everything in his path if he desires." The cacique took a slow breath. "I have seen Huracan raze forests and bash mountains, suck grown people into the sea, and pull babies from their mother's arms."

The fire shrunk back a moment, then returned with full force.

"Why does he do it?" Corinne asked.

"Why?" the cacique repeated. "People have driven themselves crazy and hurt those around them trying to understand the intention of gods. We can never know. But we are bound to listen."

"I never heard about Huracan before today," Corinne said.

"He has slept for a long time," the cacique explained. "But he is ancient as the creatures that roam the forests and live deep beneath the waters of this island."

"The jumbies," Corinne said.

"And people's memories are short," the old man continued. "Once years and years ago there were only the jumbies, or so they thought. They fought with each other over who had the most power, over who would rule. Some jumbies wanted to rule from the land. Others from the sea. Some wanted to rule from the sky. The sky jumbies got Huracan's attention. This was his domain. As the three factions fought, swirling the sea, rumbling the land, and whipping up the air, Huracan woke up and rose high above them. He raged. His winds parted and tossed the sea and every creature inside it. He left fish gasping for air on land that had been sucked dry of water. He stripped every leaf from every tree, and plucked each fruit from the branches. Then his winds pulled trees up at the root and flattened entire forests. He screamed into the air and knocked any flying creature back down to earth, pinning them there, broken and unable to get away.

"He ruled them all. There was no jumbie that could stand against him. Defeated, they agreed Huracan was the strongest. So to keep them in their places, Huracan made them swear a pact that they would each keep to their domain, land, sea, and air, and not fight anymore among themselves. And then he returned to his sleep.

"But now . . ." The cacique stared into the flame and sighed.

The fire wasn't warming Corinne anymore. She felt the cold of the rain as if she were standing in the water. She thought about Severine, who had left the land and was lost now beneath the waves. Corinne had made that happen. She thought about Mama D'Leau, whose opal allowed her to move from water to land. Corinne had delivered that stone to Mama D'Leau.

"I didn't know there was an agreement between the jumbies," Corinne whispered.

"Ignorance of the facts does not change them," the cacique said. He stood slowly and the blanket slipped off his shoulders. A lick of flame reached toward the fallen blanket as if to destroy it, but the fire righted itself before touching the fabric. The cacique was smaller than Corinne had imagined, and his hair looked different now, peppered with gray and tight, like cornrows twisted with leaves and twigs. He was bare from the waist up, but what Corinne had thought were pants were the hairy legs of a goat.

"Papa Bois," she said.

"Corinne," said the jumbie.

"Is there something we can do to stop Huracan? Is that why you are here?"

"We must wait for him to do his ill, and hope we are still standing when he has satisfied himself."

"He will destroy the island," Corinne said.

"That he will," Papa Bois agreed.

"You're just going to sit here by the fire and watch the storm?"

"What would you have me try?" Papa Bois asked. "I am rooted to this ground. Would you ask me to fly? To swim? To rage against a god I can't even reach?"

"Mama D'Leau can swim," Corinne said. "She can help."

"She is being tossed in the sea this minute," he said. "She can barely help herself. Besides, you know very well that she is not likely to help others."

"That isn't true," Corinne said. "She helped Ellie and the other mermaids."

A smile played at Papa Bois's mouth. "She did. But it was a different situation. Who would master the sky, Corinne?" he asked. Papa Bois moved away from the fire, but Corinne moved closer to it.

She bit her lip. It tasted funny and she spat out into the flame. Fire burst upward with a spray of sparks, lighting up Corinne and the jumbie and casting Papa Bois's shadow against the wall.

"I met a woman when we were coming up the mountain—"

"A frail old woman is not going to be of help," Papa Bois said.

"How do you know she was old and frail?" Corinne asked.

Papa Bois looked at her with one eyebrow cocked. "How do you think I know?"

Corinne scanned her memory for some hint that Papa Bois had been with them on the journey, but no one had seemed even slightly like him, though now she knew he could change his appearance.

"If there is nothing to be done, why did you tell me that story?" Corinne asked. "What does it matter if no one can help?"

Papa Bois shook his head. "No one," he muttered. "'*No one.*' Is that what I said?"

"I don't understand."

"Because you don't listen." He let out a sharp breath.

Corinne looked at him for a long moment, blinking, trying to understand.

"Who did I say it to?" The ground rumbled beneath him. "Who?" he shouted.

"You told it to me, to Corinne," she said.

"You," Papa Bois said.

Corinne looked down at herself. She was standing in the middle of the fire. Flames licked at her body. But it was not exactly her body. Her skin was gone, leaving only her raw flesh, red like the fire and slick as the rain. A scream bubbled up inside her and exploded like mud from an erupting volcano.

15

A Long Way Down

Corinne tried to move away from the flames, but she couldn't. She felt like she was separate from the fire, but also part of it all at once. Papa Bois watched from a few feet away at first, but as she panicked, he pulled her out by the hand, singeing some of his fur in the process. Several licks of fire came with Corinne, covering her entire body in low orange flames. She pulled away, worried she might set Papa Bois ablaze, but he was unharmed. She wanted to ask what was happening, but she couldn't find her voice.

The old jumbie led Corinne back to the house. Her skin lay on the pile of covers. What she had thought were shrugged-off sheets was her own body's covering. It lay in a sloppy pile of brown with black braids crowning the top, folded into the shirt and pants she had been wearing.

"Touch it," Papa Bois said.

Corinne looked at the flames on her body and how they threw light around the room, across the faces of her friends and Aunty Lu. She could have burned them all. The whole house. The entire village.

"Touch your skin!" Papa Bois commanded. He took her hand and moved it carefully. The moment her finger touched her own slack flesh, it wrapped around her, clothes and all. It was as simple and easy as slipping back between the sheets. Corinne felt instantly cooler, and weaker, like a snuffed-out candle.

Papa Bois walked slowly back out into the rain, as if time didn't matter at all. He looked up into the sky. Another lightning flash illuminated the clouds. The outline of a body appeared in light and shadow, and the bolt of lightning shot out of its arm. Every line was sharp and pointed directly at Corinne, like a blade approaching its target.

When the lightning ended, Papa Bois had vanished.

• • •

"Wake up, Corinne," Dru said.

Corinne felt like she was floating far off, and Dru's voice wavered in the distance, hard to catch on to, like the tail of a kite. Dru called again and Corinne opened her eyes.

"You're missing breakfast," Dru said. "The boys are already up, and you know them. They will eat everything."

Corinne squinted at the bright sky outside. The salty scent of freshly cooked eggs mixed with the fresh, wormy smell of rain-sodden dirt. Her body felt wrecked, like the mountain itself had rolled over her. She gasped and lifted the covers. She was whole, not the raw creature of flesh and blood who had stood in the fire last night and not the fire creature that had returned to the house. She was herself. Corinne.

"Did you have a bad dream?" Dru asked.

Corinne shook her head. It had not been a dream. She was sure of that. It was no wonder that her body felt like it had been turned inside out and back again. It had been.

"Then what?" Dru asked.

"I don't feel well," Corinne said.

Dru put her hand on Corinne's forehead. Corinne cringed, expecting Dru to pull back burned, but nothing happened. "You don't feel hot," she said. Then she looked in Corinne's eyes for a few seconds, her brow knit with worry. Corinne imagined that Dru was mimicking what her own mother did when any of the Rootsingh children were ill, but she knew that what she had wasn't detectable by the usual methods. "Maybe Aunty Lu will let you lie down longer," Dru said. "I'll tell her you're feeling poorly."

"Thank you," Corinne said. She rolled over again and went back to sleep. When she woke the next time, she heard people walking outside her room, and the sun was brighter than before.

"Good morning!" Aunty Lu's voice boomed through the small house. "I thought you were dead away." She laid a plate of eggs, steaming hot and fragrant, next to Corinne's head. "Eat. You will need your strength."

"For what?" Corinne asked.

Aunty Lu looked surprised. "Don't you want to get back to your father? Your friend is anxious to find her family."

Corinne's face flushed. In all her thoughts that morning, she hadn't given a single thought to her papa below. "Yes. Of course."

"It's going to be a long day for you if you want to go back down the mountain." Aunty Lu exited the house, and Corinne caught a glimpse of her friends outside, playing in the slippery grass with other children, kicking up red mud. Dru had picked up her tunic and was running from a much smaller child. Malik was in the middle of a scuffle of giggling boys and girls. Bouki stood off to the side, watching them and laughing.

The boys looked so comfortable. They looked like they belonged.

Corinne ate quickly and strode out of the house. "We have to go," she said.

Dru immediately came to her side. "I'm ready."

Bouki looked at her but didn't move.

"We have to go," Corinne said again.

"You just woke up and you're barking orders?" Bouki shook his head.

"Uncle Hugo is going to be worried about you," Corinne said loudly.

Malik and the other children looked up, as did a few of the adults nearby, including Aunty Lu.

Bouki's eyes narrowed. "Don't you think I know that?"

"Well?"

"You're the one who's been sleeping all morning!" Bouki said.

"She wasn't feeling well," Dru said.

Bouki shrugged and called roughly to Malik. "Come on. It's time to go."

Malik shook his head. He pressed back into the little muddy knot of playmates and planted his feet.

"What do you mean, 'no'?" Bouki said. "We have to go home."

Malik shook his head again. He squared his jaw and shoulders.

"Hugo will be waiting," Bouki said.

Malik slackened a little. He didn't move, but he didn't shake his head, either.

Aunty Lu approached the two of them, smiling. "You know where we are," she said. "You can always come back for him." She put her hands on Malik's shoulders and faced Bouki.

"I don't know you," Bouki said. "I won't leave my brother here."

Malik puffed out his chest and jutted his chin toward his brother now that he had Aunty Lu on his side.

Bouki turned to Corinne and Dru. "I can't leave him here."

"We can't get down without you," Corinne said. "We'll get lost."

"Not so," Aunty Lu said. "There is another way down the mountain. You won't even need a guide. And it's the fastest way down . . . well, other than falling."

Corinne felt a twinge in her stomach. It was a strange thing to say. She looked to Dru for agreement, but Dru was staring wide-eyed at Aunty Lu. Corinne pulled Bouki aside. "You're going to stay here?" she whispered. "You don't know these people."

"They're family."

Corinne felt the wind knocked out of her. "Just like that? They left you all by yourselves."

"They looked for us, Corinne."

"Not well enough!" Her voice rose and caught the attention of everyone nearby. "They should have looked longer," she added quietly.

Bouki put a hand on her shoulder. "They're family. You give family a chance to be forgiven."

"Don't worry," Aunty Lu assured them, stepping close to Corinne and Bouki. "The journey down is perfectly safe." She nodded at a couple of people in the crowd who stepped forward, each holding a bag. They handed one to Corinne and one to Dru, then stepped back. "There's food and water in there in case you get hungry," Aunty Lu said. "Keep them tied at the top. They're waterproof."

Corinne looked pointedly at Dru again. Dru still didn't notice.

The girls put the bags over their shoulders as Aunty Lu stepped around Malik and put her heavy hands on them. "I'll show you the way."

Aunty Lu led them through the village doorway and then down the stone steps. They followed the brow of the mountain, going around its curve until the sun began to sink again and they came to another set of stairs, narrower than the first. "Nearly there," she said. The stairs ended at a thin shelf, beyond which was a steep slope. It was bare in spots where trees had been knocked over. Corinne traced the sky from horizon to horizon for storm clouds, but it was clear and bright blue. Maybe Huracan had vented all of his anger.

"Stay close to the side," Aunty Lu warned. She pressed herself against the rocks and inched forward. Corinne and Dru held hands as they did the same. A warm, gentle breeze tugged at their clothes and hair. But soon they were in a wider spot, bald of grass, with only a few scrubby branches poking through the hard ground.

"Here," Aunty Lu said.

"Where?" Corinne asked. There was nothing there. Up ahead was a flat rock face that Corinne was sure she couldn't climb up or go down.

Aunty Lu pulled a lever and a large wicker basket descended from a ledge above them. It was woven around a metal frame and attached to a rope that sloped downward and into the tree line. The basket was large enough for a single grown-up to fit inside, or two small girls.

"Nope," said Dru.

Aunty Lu laughed. "You will be safe," she promised. "Smaller ones than you have ridden on this."

"Where does it lead?" Corinne asked.

"No," Dru said again.

"The pitch lake," Aunty Lu said. She walked around the basket, checking its seams and tugging at the rope and pulley it was attached to.

"Is that close to where we came on the mountain?"

"It's the other side. But it's the quickest way down." Aunty Lu held the basket steady in front of the girls.

Dru shook her head.

"You can swim, right?" Aunty Lu asked.

"Yes," Corinne said.

"Nope," Dru said.

Aunty Lu looked surprised.

"She'll be fine," Corinne said.

"Good," Aunty Lu said. She opened up a small door on one side of the basket and helped the girls inside.

Dru clutched Corinne's arm.

"It will be fast," Corinne said.

"How is that better?" Dru asked.

Aunty Lu latched the door behind them, gave the basket a push, and they hurtled down the side of the mountain.

16

The Pitch Lake

D ru knelt, forehead firmly planted against the bottom of the basket, arms hugging herself. Corinne crouched too, but found a chink in the weaving and peeked through. The mountain looked as if a giant had stomped across it, leaving the red dirt exposed like wounds. Mudslides trailed like tear tracks. In some places, the mud still tumbled down slowly enough that Corinne could see exactly what it would destroy next.

As they approached the end of the line, scattered wood beams and the galvanized roofs of houses came into sight. One house had fallen to the side, leaving the four posts of its foundation and a set of stairs climbing to nothing but

< 113 >

air. Curtains billowed from the broken windows as the sideways house stared unblinkingly up at the sky that had brought it down.

A smattering of cows, a few goats and dogs, and some fast-flapping chickens picked their way through the wreckage, nosing what was left of the houses, the trees, the demolished gardens, and the impassable roads.

Corinne's stomach twisted as she thought of her papa and the others in the caves. Were they safe enough?

The basket dipped low and slowed. Corinne stood on her tiptoes to look over the top. They were descending into a valley that Corinne had never seen before. Around them were hills scoured clean of vegetation by Huracan. Beneath lay a lake like glass that reflected the sky so perfectly, for a moment Corinne thought they were headed back up.

The basket skimmed the lake, ruffling its glassy surface and stirring up the strong scent of sulfur.

"What is that?" Dru screwed up her face and put a hand over her nose and mouth.

"It's the water," Corinne said.

"We have to swim in that?" Dru asked.

Corinne looked around. "There's no other way out. Maybe it's not so bad."

The basket rose slightly, slowed to a stop, and then swung back. It came to rest hovering just over the top of the water. Corinne opened the door, holding on to the metal frame that attached it to the pulley and rope, and jumped down. She splashed in a few inches of water, but her feet hit bottom almost immediately, and then began to sink into gummy ground. She pulled one foot out, but her sandal stuck in the gunk at the bottom of the lake. When she bent to retrieve it, her foot slipped from under her and she landed on her back. The ground began to swallow her. Dru jumped down, grabbed Corinne's arm, and tried to pull her up, but she also slipped in the muck. Corinne was completely beneath the water. She twisted onto her stomach and got up on her knees. Once again, the soft lake bed pulled at her, but at last she managed to get her feet under her and step away.

"You can't stay in one place for long," she said.

"We need to get away from here," Dru agreed. She held the bag from Aunty Lu firmly and took off at a waddling run, prying her feet up and out of the water with every step. "You were right, it's not so bad!" she said, but with her next step, she went straight under the surface with a huge splash.

"Dru!" Corinne moved to where Dru had sunk and found the bottom curving downward. She inched forward with her feet and moved her hands beneath the glassy water, hoping to feel her friend. When she was submerged to her chest, the slope sharpened. Corinne tried to grip with her toes, but she slid deeper.

She took a deep breath as she slipped under the surface of the murky lake.

Everything below was a blurred yellowish green. Corinne could see more now than from above the surface, but not by much. Her foot touched a little lip of ground and she used it to push herself forward, looking for any shape that resembled Dru. Corinne's hands moved in large slow arcs in front of her, trying to feel for Dru, more of the mucky ground, anything that might be in the way.

At last, out of the corner of her eye, Corinne saw something flick, like a hand waving. She turned toward it and touched a small sandal. She kept moving in that direction until a fluttering piece of cloth brushed her hand. She grabbed it and pulled hard. Dru crashed against her and her eyes widened with surprise. Corinne kicked to the surface, dragging Dru by the end of her tunic.

As she breached the water, Corinne took a huge gulping breath, then pulled Dru out. Dru coughed and sputtered. They swam back toward the basket and pulled up onto the sticky black ground.

"It's all over you," Dru said.

Corinne looked at herself. Shiny black tar streaked her skin and clothes. She tried to pick it off, but it stuck on her fingers and clung beneath her nails.

"You too," Corinne said.

Dru rubbed at the hem of her tunic where black tar stuck to the embroidery. "It's really ruined now," she said.

Corinne got up and pulled Dru with her. Together they waded through the lake, feeling their way with their toes to make sure there was solid ground beneath them. With every step, the pitch sucked their feet down, so they had to pull with force to move forward. It was slow and frustrating, but better than being swallowed by the lake.

They got closer to what looked like solid ground with a few patches of grass growing up between rocks. Relieved, Corinne leapt toward one of the rocks. Her toes hit the surface, but the rest of her foot came down in soft, slick tar. She teetered on the edge, trying to keep her balance.

"Corinne!" Dru shouted.

Corinne felt her friend's hands groping at her as she slipped down a narrow shaft between two huge lumps of tar, barely splashing as she knifed through the water. Dru's face peered down, large panicked eyes atop a shadowy body. Corinne could read Dru's expression clearly, but it was obvious that Dru couldn't see her at all.

Corinne spread her arms and legs to slow her descent. She slowed, then kicked upward again, focusing on the sliver of light that separated her from Dru, and from air, but the farther up she went, the thinner the sliver became, until it disappeared entirely. She reached up and touched the underside of a layer of tar. She tore at it with her fingers, sure she could somehow peel herself free, but it was huge and solid, and her efforts didn't bring her any closer to the light, or to the air that she was beginning to desperately need.

Corinne turned. She would have to find another way up. But all around her, the ground was shifting like a huge, lumbering creature. She dove again as the black pitch coated even more of the surface. She looked for any opening. Every time she saw light and swam to it, the path closed.

Corinne put her hands to her neck, feeling for her mama's necklace. It had saved her before. She forgot it was gone.

Her vision dimmed. She needed air. She reached a hand toward the only light she could find, but the surface was no closer.

There was only one thing she could do. Darkness closed in around Corinne's vision. With her last breath, she murmured a name.

17

A Quick Rescue

Corinne's call rippled out through the brackish water, undulating over the tar hills and stretching out to sea.

It was enough.

The next thing she felt was the rough scrape of scales against her body and a pair of soft arms buoying her up. She was pushed into the air, where she gulped breath and sputtered water. She fell on a soft bank right at Dru's feet.

"You're alive!" Dru shouted.

Two mermaids pushed themselves halfway out of the water next to Corinne. Their faces were deep brown with dark eyes, and their long, thick hair was braided in dozens of plaits that fell over their shoulders and down their backs. The smaller of the two mermaids lifted herself out of the water to the dark yellow scales that began at her waist, and slapped Corinne on the back. More water sprayed out of Corinne's mouth.

"There now, you're fine and we're covered in pitch. It's going to be impossible to get this out." The other mermaid, Addie, flicked her green tail out of the water and rubbed at its scales, but the pitch only smeared against her shimmering body, dulling the color.

Corinne spat up the last of the water and took a deep breath. Her lungs and throat burned, but the air was fresh and sweet. "Thank you," she said.

"You know I will always come," Sisi said. "I promised."

"What about my papa?" Corinne asked. "Have you seen him?"

"I'm sure he's fine," Sisi said. "Don't worry."

"How do you know?" Addie asked. She turned to Corinne. "What she means is he's not dead in the water."

Sisi flicked her tail and splashed dirty water onto Addie's head and arms. "That was a terrible thing to say!"

"Now it's in my hair, too!" Addie complained. "It's true. You can only track Pierre in the water," Addie said, picking a piece of pitch out of a long, thin plait. "What is the point of lying?"

"How come there are only two of you?" Dru asked. "Where's Noyi?"

"You know how Noyi is," Addie said. "You land fish are not her favorite."

"What are the two of *you* doing here?" Sisi asked. "It's a long way from your homes."

"When the second storm hit we went up into the mountains," Corinne explained.

Sisi looked revolted. "Is there any water up there?"

"Not enough to swim in," Dru said.

Addie shuddered. "Disgusting."

"When the storm was over, they sent us back down in a basket," Corinne said. She turned to point to the basket, but it was gone. The rope that had brought them down swung empty.

"Who are *they*?" Sisi asked.

"There are people who live high up in the mountain."

"They are Bouki and Malik's family," Dru added.

"Well . . ." Corinne said.

"You don't believe Aunty Lu?" Dru asked.

"It's just that she got rid of us so fast. Didn't you see how she had the bags prepared to send us off? Just two of them? Like she knew the boys weren't going anywhere?"

Dru looked skeptical. "She was nice. She took care of us."

"She pushed us down the side of a mountain in a

tiny basket that ended at a lake that nearly drowned us." Corinne cocked an eye at Dru and waited.

Dru frowned. "You wanted to go in that basket," she said. "You said it would be fine."

The mermaids looked at the girls, then each other, and broke into laughter.

"Never mind," Corinne said. She folded her arms tightly around her chest. "We need to get home. Can you help?"

"I can take Dru to the lagoon," Addie offered. "That's close to your village, isn't it?"

"But my family is still in the mountains," Dru said.

"The rain stopped. They would go back home," Corinne said.

"Not without me."

"Somebody would return to the house, or to the village. It's your best choice."

"And it's the closest I can get you," Addie said.

"I will take you to your beach," Sisi said to Corinne. "We can be there very quickly."

Corinne turned to Dru. "I will come and find you after I have talked to Papa and the white witch."

The mermaids looked at each other, and a small, whimpering sound escaped Addie's throat. Sisi slapped her on the back and it turned into a cough.

"What is it?" Corinne asked.

Sisi played nervously with the end of a plait. "You mentioned the white witch."

"I need to talk to her," Corinne said. "I need to find out what she knows about Huracan, and those people we met on the mountain."

"I . . . I don't know about any mountainfolk," Sisi said. "But . . . the witch . . ."

Addie moved forward and touched Corinne's hand. "The white witch is gone," she said. "The water took her."

Corinne wasn't sure if it was the ground moving beneath her feet or the news of the white witch's death that made her unsteady. Dru took her elbow and helped her find her balance.

"I'm sorry, Corinne," Dru said.

"She was quite old," Addie said.

"She was strong," Corinne said. "She was tough. She's probably seen a hundred hurricanes like this one and survived. You're wrong. You're wrong! She's going to be in the swamp. I know it."

"Corinne." Dru put her arms around her friend and let her sob against her shoulder.

"Are you sure?" Corinne asked, muffled by Dru's kurta.

"Yes. And I think in the end she was at peace," Sisi said. "We didn't sense her struggle."

"And, she also . . ." Addie began, but once again, Sisi shut her up with a slap of her tail.

"Who will help me now?" Corinne asked, wiping her face and smearing pitch on her cheeks.

"We can help each other," Sisi said.

Corinne looked at the mermaids bobbing in the water. Thanks to her papa, she had learned to detect even a flicker of worry in the furrow of a brow, or the tightness of a cheek. "Something else is wrong, isn't it?"

"Mama D'Leau is in trouble," Addie said. "We can't get to her. The water is holding her captive. Every time we try to get close, the current pushes us away."

"But the storm is over," Dru said. "The water should be calm."

"It's Huracan," Corinne said. "It must be."

Dru shook her head. "No."

"What else, then?" Corinne asked. "Huracan controls the storms, and he can blow the currents any way he likes."

Dru looked into the clear blue sky. "I thought it was over."

"So did I," Corinne said.

"Who is Huracan?" the mermaids asked together.

"Huracan is the reason for the storms, and probably the reason you can't get to Mama D'Leau," Corinne said.

"Why would he trap her?" Sisi asked. "He's hurting her."

Corinne could have pointed out that Mama D'Leau was not known for mercy. How many fishermen and swimmers had she turned to stone on a whim? For how many hundreds of years? Many would cheer to know that Mama D'Leau was finally being kept at bay. Not long ago, Corinne might have been one of those people, but now? Now, the idea that something was stronger than the strongest jumbie she knew, and that it was ripping the whole island apart, filled her with terror.

"Mama D'Leau had an agreement that she didn't keep," Corinne said. "She was supposed to stay in the water, but she didn't."

"The witch sent a message before she died," Sisi said.

"She said that Mama D'Leau would need help," Addie continued.

"We think she meant from you," Sisi finished.

"I have to check on my papa first," Corinne said. "Then we will see about Mama D'Leau. Maybe she knows what I'm supposed to do."

"You can't go alone," Dru said.

"I won't," Corinne promised. "There will be enough time to check on our families and meet on the beach. Won't there?"

Once again, the mermaids exchanged a glance, but Corinne couldn't read it.

Corinne dove into the water next to Sisi. Dru went in more carefully and took Addie's hand.

"I'll see you soon," Corinne said.

Addie took Dru by the waist and disappeared.

Sisi twined her fingers with Corinne's. "You lied to your friend," she said.

"I don't know what you mean."

"You are not the only one who can tell when someone is hiding something." She brought a cold finger to Corinne's furrowed brow.

"There are things my friends don't understand," Corinne explained.

Sisi gave an understanding nod. Corinne sunk below the surface. The two of them raced off through the shifting pitch hills, cutting around, under, and over them until they made it out to sea.

Corinne felt the difference between the lake water and the sea immediately. It was clearer for one, cooler, and then there was the sting of salt in her eyes. She tapped Sisi's arm and pointed up. Sisi swam to the surface so that Corinne could take a breath.

"How come I can't breathe underwater like last time?"

"Mama D'Leau made that possible," Sisi said. "Now it's just us and we don't have her magic."

Corinne gulped air and Sisi pulled her around the island until they came to the small beach at Corinne's fishing village.

Corinne immediately looked up to the house, but from that distance, all she could see was that it was still standing. Parts of the roof had blown off, and at least one window was flapping open and closed. That meant Corinne's papa was probably not at home.

Sisi pushed Corinne close to shore. The water was filled with floating coconuts, branches, and the sharp fronds of palm leaves. Where it was shallow enough to stand Corinne dropped her feet. Broken shells, stones, and chunks of gritty sand dug into her toes. As she walked out to the beach, she nearly impaled her foot on a nail embedded in a plank of wood covered in chipped pink paint. Corinne picked it up.

All the homes on the shore were in bad shape. Roofs were torn apart, wall boards pried loose. The beach was littered with debris.

Down the shore, Laurent walked through the sand, picking up bits of board, lamps, dishes, tossing some and putting others into a sack he had slung on one shoulder.

"Laurent!" Corinne called. She jogged to him, stepping carefully to avoid all the debris. She handed him the piece of his wall. He added it to the sack. "Have you seen my papa?"

Laurent shook his head. He picked at a lump of tar that clung to the hem of her shirt. "Where are you coming from?"

"The pitch lake, and then . . ." Corinne pointed out to sea, where Sisi was still bobbing among the waves. Laurent raised his eyebrows.

"And what about your family?" Corinne asked.

"Everyone is well," Laurent said. But he looked exhausted.

"Corinne!" Abner, Laurent's little brother, ran up. He hugged her around the waist, nearly toppling her.

"Hi Abner," Corinne said. "Are you helping Laurent?" He nodded enthusiastically.

"Do you want me to come to your house with you?" Laurent offered.

"No, thank you," Corinne said.

She climbed the hill, keeping her eyes glued to the house at the top. With every step closer, she could see more damage. The fence had blown over, and the gate was gone. Some of the planks that had covered the windows had fallen away, and the windows themselves were open and broken. The ones closest to the sea were loose on their hinges and swinging free.

Corinne went all the way around the yard. Most of the garden was bare. Even the half-drum that held the chives looked like something had scooped out all the dirt, leaving just a few frayed sprigs, their edges blowing in the wind like hair. She found the gate tangled in the branches of her orange tree, whose bright fruits were strewn on the ground. Orange ones, yellow ones, green ones were all bumped and bruised in the dirt. She picked up the closest one and breathed in its sweet, sharp scent. It reminded her that not everything was entirely ruined. She kept it in her hand as she entered the house. The door still worked.

The inside of the house was rain-soaked, but appeared to be intact. Her papa had put down bowls and pots to catch water, she guessed, when the roof only had a few holes in it. Now it gaped open and the vessels were useless.

Corinne splashed through the water-logged floor and put the orange on the table. All the familiar smells of the house—the oiled wood, the mild candle wax, the strong scent of the sea, even the pungent orange—were no comfort. The house felt emptier than it had ever seemed when her papa was fishing on the sea.

She thought about walking into town. Her papa would be returning from that way, and she might find Uncle Hugo and hear how they had made out in the storm, but the thought that she might find nothing, or worse, that she would find her papa had suffered the same fate as the white witch, nicked at her heart and kept her rooted to the spot.

Besides, her papa had always told her to wait for him at the house in case of emergencies. She could do that. While she waited, she would start repairing what she could.

Corinne moved through the house, picking up fallen pieces of furniture—the rocking chair that sat by the window overlooking the sea and the small table where they ate their meals. She got the lamps off the floor, swept away the broken glass, and sopped up the water and oil with towels. Everything that had survived was put back in place. Reparable items, like the oil lamps that needed new glass, the ripped curtains that she could re-sew, and her papa's spare fishing rod that could be restrung, she placed carefully on the table. The rest went into a large dustbin in the backyard.

The bin was too large and heavy for Corinne to move. Her papa would have to take care of it when he came home. Worry pricked at her, and she strained her ears, hoping to hear his footsteps. She only heard the sounds of the fishing village cleaning below. As she tried to stifle that worry, another thought crept in, the agreement that Papa Bois had told her about. Huracan had forced the land jumbies, water jumbies, and air jumbies to live separately. But Severine had fallen into the sea, and then Mama D'Leau had gotten the opal that made it possible for her to walk on land. Then Corinne had taken Severine away to a far ocean. It was no wonder Huracan was still angry, and his storm was still brewing. But there was nothing Corinne could do about it now. Everything she had tried so far had made things worse.

She turned back to the house.

After the floors were clear, she moved to the bedrooms, pulling sodden sheets off the beds and dragging the mattresses out to dry in the sun. She had just gotten her papa's mattress outside and leaned it against the house when she heard a noise.

"Corinne!"

"Papa?" Corinne dashed inside and into Pierre's arms.

"Where have you been? The rain stopped hours ago."

"We couldn't get back down the same way, Papa."

"What happened?"

Corinne quickly explained about their night with Aunty Lu and the basket ride down to the pitch lake. She left out the part where she and Dru nearly drowned, and how Aunty Lu had given them no warning, but she told Pierre that Sisi had brought her to the house.

"Are the boys with you?" Pierre asked.

Hugo was just making his way in, jogging slowly and looking around with an expectant smile on his face.

"No," Corinne said. "The boys are still up the mountain."

Hugo's face fell.

"People have been coming out of the mountain all morning," Hugo said. "They must still be helping everyone."

"Yes," Corinne said a little too quickly.

"What good boys!" Hugo said. He clapped his large hands together, causing his body to ripple with joy. "My boys!" He beamed. "They will be hungry when they get back." He looked at Corinne for confirmation.

"You know they are always hungry, Uncle Hugo," she said.

"Well, you and Corinne are reunited, Pierre. I will go

wait for my boys." Hugo left without another word, whistling as he walked down the path and onto the road.

"Do you want to tell me what really happened with Bouki and Malik?" Pierre asked when Hugo was out of earshot.

"They found their real family," Corinne whispered. "Aunty Lu didn't ask us to call her that because she helped us. It's because she is their real aunt."

Pierre sighed and looked at the door where Hugo had stood just moments before.

Corinne swallowed. "I'm glad you're safe, Papa," she said. Pierre held her tightly, but after a few seconds Corinne pushed out of his hug. He frowned, waiting for her to explain. "I have to leave."

"What do you mean?"

"I have to help Mama D'Leau."

"Now?" Pierre asked.

"She's trapped under the water, and the mermaids can't get to her. You told me the first storm was unusual." Corinne waited as Pierre nodded. "And then the second storm came."

"That was unexpected," he agreed. "But now it's over."

Corinne shook her head. "It's not happening by chance. There is a god, Huracan, who is causing all of it."

Pierre chuckled. "Hugo told me the boys' story. But there is no such thing, Corinne."

"There weren't any jumbies either," Corinne said.

"And the fish-folk were just a story we made up . . . until they weren't."

Pierre's face clouded. "A god?" he asked. He passed a hand over his dreadlocked hair as he stared out the back door, over the horizon.

"Papa," Corinne said sharply. "I have to help Mama D'Leau. She is trapped in the water. Only Huracan could do that. And that means it's not over. Maybe there isn't a storm right now, but something else will come, and there is no one else who can help her."

Pierre shook his head and grasped her arm firmly. "No. You will not. You are safe here. There is nothing you can do to help."

"Papa!" Corinne tried to pull away. "I promised the mermaids. They are counting on me."

"You are a little girl," Pierre said softly but firmly. "You will not leave. You will be injured. Or worse!"

"What would you do, Papa, to save your family?"

Pierre looked surprised, and then his face fell. "Anything. Everything. But they are not your family, Corinne."

"They are, Papa," Corinne said. "They were my mama's people. So they are mine, too."

"Don't tell me about your mama, Corinne!" Pierre shouted. He let go of Corinne's arm roughly.

Corinne rubbed the spot he had held. It was fine, but his words had left a mark.

"She would have helped, Papa," Corinne said.

"She would," he said. "She did! And what did it get her?" Pierre held on to the back of a chair and his shoulders slumped.

"What do you mean?" Corinne asked.

"This isn't about your mother," Pierre said. "It's about you. Your choices. Your actions. Maybe I raised you to be too independent, spending all my time on the sea. So you don't consider how what you do has an effect."

Corinne stiffened. All she had done lately was worry about what happened because of her actions.

"You take the boat into dangerous waters. You climb a cliff over sharp rocks. You bargain with jumbies and cross the ocean. You disappear beneath the waves. You run out in the eye of a hurricane." His voice was thin and raw. "You tempt fate, Corinne. How long until fate catches up? How long until you get hurt?"

Corinne swallowed hard over a painful lump in her throat. "Papa, I'm sorry."

"I told you there was another storm like this, one that you couldn't possibly remember."

Corinne's lip quivered. "Yes, Papa."

"It was just as terrible as this one, with lightning cutting across the sky. And it took your mama."

Corinne felt like something hard had lodged in her throat, making it difficult to breathe.

"The lightning struck your mama," he said. "She

had been feeling unwell before the storm. She couldn't survive."

Corinne sank into her papa's chest and let him wrap his arms around her. "You never told me," she said.

Pierre took a deep breath. "You cannot go," he said. "Do you see?"

"I have to go, anyway, Papa," Corinne said. "This time, the god is not going to stop until everything and everyone on this island is broken."

"If you go, I might lose you."

Corinne held her papa's face in her hands. "If I don't go, we will lose everything."

18

The Other Mermaid

C orinne's toes had barely touched the froth at the break of the waves when two mermaids bobbed out of the water. She swam out to meet them, and Sisi grabbed her hand and dragged her into the sea. Corinne took a last glimpse at Pierre, who stood on shore, forlorn, before she was pulled under.

Sisi's fins and tail flashed yellow with red at the tip. Addie swam ahead of them, a bright green slash in the water. They moved past the waving coral reef, which looked like it had been ripped apart, then past another, older reef farther out that lay bleached as bones, broken and scattered in the golden sea sand. Corinne pointed to the surface, indicating she needed more air, but this time Sisi and Addie didn't notice. They kept moving, around the skeleton of the ancient coral reef to the far side where Mama D'Leau lay coiled up in her own tail. Corinne went limp at the sight of the powerful jumbie lying in the sand like a washed-up fish. Sisi tugged her along. But as they got close, the water pushed against them, hurtling them away from the old reef with a spray of bubbles and sand. Corinne used that moment to break free of Sisi's grasp and kick to the surface for a breath.

Sisi and Addie came up with her, as well as the third mermaid, Noyi.

"Took you long enough," Noyi snapped. She was thicker than the other two, with her hair coiled into an elaborate bun of plaits on top of her head.

"She was looking for her papa," Sisi explained.

Noyi rolled her eyes. "And all the while, I have been here, trying to get Mama out."

"I came as quickly as I could," Corinne said.

"So what do we do now?" Addie asked. "We can't get close to her no matter what we do."

"What have you tried?" Corinne asked.

Noyi put her hands on her scaly dark blue hips. "How many ways is there to get to a person?" she snapped. "We have been trying to swim to her."

"From the front always?" Corinne asked.

"The reef is at her back," Sisi said. "With the pull that

strong, we'd get gouged on the old coral trying to reach her from behind."

The cut on Corinne's leg from the time she had climbed the cliff began to tingle. She rubbed it. "You aren't used to having to hang on to things," Corinne said. "You have to hold on with your hands and your feet."

"Feet." Noyi pursed her lips and glared at her.

Corinne looked down at the mermaid's waving tail. "Right. Well, I know how to hang on. I've done it hundreds of times while climbing," Corinne said. "One of you could put me in the coral, and I'll get to her from the back."

"What makes you think this Huracan won't notice you?" Addie asked.

"You'll distract him," Corinne said.

"But then the current will take you," Sisi said.

"That's when I have to hang on the hardest."

Sisi's face brightened. Addie shrugged, but Noyi looked even more irritated.

"How long do you think that will take?" Noyi asked. "Can you suddenly breathe underwater, land fish?"

"Land fish!" Addie snorted. "She's a cascadura!"

"Swimming in the mud!" Noyi said, laughing.

Corinne bristled. "Do you want my help or not?"

The mermaids quieted down.

"If this doesn't work, we will think of something else," Corinne said. Without waiting for the mermaids, she took a gulp of air and went under, swimming for the dead reef.

Sisi pulled Corinne along and dropped her in the middle of the coral, as close to Mama D'Leau as she could get. She swam off, joining Addie and Noyi, who had gone around the reef. Together they tried to approach Mama D'Leau from the front again. Hopefully their actions would distract Huracan from the small girl hiding in the stiff coral.

As soon as the mermaids got close, the current stirred. The water felt like it was draining in one direction, pulling Corinne with it. She held on tight to the coral even though it dug into her hands and feet. When the current had pushed the mermaids away, the pressure lowered. Corinne pressed forward, picking her way over the razor-sharp shards. She stayed low and moved as slowly as she could, but she was quickly running out of breath.

Corinne's foot slipped and caught the edge of a broken brain coral. She yelped bubbles, losing precious air. The water rushed at her again. Her feet flew out from under her, pulled into a vortex. She held on tight. Her left hand bled from the coral, but she didn't let go. The water built pressure against her, squeezing out what little air she had left in her lungs. The coral broke in her hand. Corinne was pried off the reef and went spinning.

Corinne felt Mama D'Leau's strong, muscled tail wrap around her and pull her down to the sand. But Corinne needed to go up toward air. The water swirled as if it was trying to pluck her from Mama D'Leau's tail.

The jumbie squeezed harder and pulled Corinne into its depth like a slowly turning screw. When Corinne was wholly engulfed in the tail, she looked directly into a pair of deep blue eyes that blinked out at her from the darkness.

So you come, then, Mama D'Leau said.

Air! Corinne managed. *Air!*

Mama D'Leau loosened her tail a little, and Corinne felt the need for air disappear from her body. The jumbie could allow anyone she wanted to breathe underwater.

Corinne paused a moment, enjoying the feeling of air-filled lungs. *Thank you,* she said. *It's Huracan who has you trapped.*

You think I don't know that? Mama D'Leau said. *You could have stayed on land if that is all you have to share.*

I think I can help.

You can't even breathe.

I could if you changed me.

And then what? Mama D'Leau asked. *You would be in the same position as those three.*

They looked out through the coils of Mama D'Leau's tail at the three mermaids swimming just outside of the swirling current.

Huracan is angry with you, but he's angry about Severine, too, Corinne said. *If I bring her back and get her on the island, he will be satisfied.*

Mama D'Leau threw her head back and laughed a long, gurgling laugh. *What you know about how Huracan feel?*

The white witch taught me about balance. And Papa Bois told me that you all had an agreement. It was broken when . . . Corinne stopped herself from saying that the agreement had been broken when Mama D'Leau sent her for the opal that allowed her to walk on land. *It doesn't matter how it was broken,* she said instead. *What matters is that I can help fix it.*

No.

Why not? Corinne asked. *Because if Severine comes back you can't be on land anymore?*

Who tell you so?

I figured it out for myself, Corinne said. She felt the muscle of the tail squeeze tight again. The space grew dark and hot, but the jumbie's cold skin pressed against her. *The opal lets you come on land, but you couldn't do that while Severine was there. She wouldn't allow it.* Corinne paused. *Wait. You got me to get rid of her for you!*

Mama D'Leau chuckled. *That was all your idea. I never tell you to pull she into the sea.*

But you made sure it was the only choice I had. Now with her gone and you walking on land, Huracan thinks there is too much chaos. Too much trouble. So he is going to put every-body back in their place the only way he knows how. Corinne lowered her voice. *I can find Severine. I can bring her back. We can have balance again.*

You would bring she back after all she do to you? Mama D'Leau asked.

She's family, Corinne said. *You give family a chance to be forgiven. And anyway, there is no other way to satisfy Huracan.*

The tail tightened around Corinne again. She was sure the pressure would crack her bones. Corinne dug her fingers into the jumbie's flesh and tried to pry her way out, but Mama D'Leau's grasp was impossible to slip. Finally, Mama D'Leau released Corinne, who floated up and out of the coils. This time there was no current pushing her away. It was almost as if Huracan himself had approved the plan. Corinne floated far above Mama D'Leau's head. When she looked down, the jumbie was freeing herself from the pale, broken coral, and the mermaids were coming to Mama D'Leau's side.

There was something else—a bright orange tail extended from Corinne's hips. Corinne felt suddenly cold as worry wrapped around her. Her eyes flicked to shore, where her papa waited. He was right. She had not considered the effect of her actions. The last time she had become a mermaid, she had forgotten her home, her friends, and her papa. Would it happen again? She wished he was close.

Mama D'Leau's tail unfurled toward Corinne. As the end straightened, a necklace slipped from its scales. Corinne caught it. It was the necklace with her mama's stone, broken and wrapped in leather to keep it together.

She rubbed her thumb on the pendant, feeling every familiar nick and crack. It wasn't her papa, but maybe it was enough.

Thank you.

You will need it when you start to forget yourself, Mama D'Leau said.

It didn't help me to remember the last time, Corinne said.

But now you know it will happen, so you can try to stop it.

19

A Cloud in the Water

Corinne hesitated only a moment to retie her mama's necklace around her throat. She popped her head above the waves to look at her papa, who stood on the beach. Saying she would come right back was the second lie she had told that day. She turned away, moving south, and followed the same path she had taken months ago when she had left the island with Severine.

She kept one hand on the necklace and repeated things she knew to be true.

I am Corinne. I live on an island with my papa.

My friends are Dru, Bouki, Malik, Laurent, and Marlene.

My oranges are the sweetest on the island.

Tante Severine is my mother's sister. She is family.

The water turned cold and Corinne's skin tightened. When the sea thickened with ice, she chased shadows, searching for Severine but finding only sharks and lumbering whales. She dove deep where the light dimmed to nearly black. Her vision changed, like a light turning on, brightening despite the darkness, so every flashing scale, every flapping fin, and every mote of sand in the depths shone brightly.

I am Corinne.

She wove through the water, slowly. She couldn't come back empty-handed. She turned in every direction and combed the cold seafloor for any sign of Severine, but there was none. In all the time since Corinne had left Severine behind, her aunt could have traveled anywhere in the world, and there was no way to track her. The water did not leave marks, and the ocean was vast.

Tante Severine is my mother's sister.

Corinne stopped and tried to consider her choices. The current pulled her a little way, depositing her near a circle of rocks stacked like misshapen vases. They were white on the outside, but the inner shafts were dark. Corinne caught one of them to stop herself from drifting farther. It was hot. She pulled her hand away and rubbed it. The current pulled her again, widening her view. It was not one small rock circle, but several of them, wide as a coral reef, and she was in the middle. Corinne pushed against the current to move back in the direction she had come from. She strained to make her way to open water.

A small, hard creature like a dark crab scrambled out from between one of the open mouths in the rocks. Then there was another, and another. They spilled out in wave after wave, like they were running from something. Panic rose in Corinne's throat. She tried to move faster. The sea trembled around her, then became still. A moment later a plume of deep gray erupted from the center of each rocky vase. Corinne watched what looked like a volcanic eruption play out in slow motion as the smoke-colored water reached toward her. It was instantly warmer, and Corinne felt more comfortable, but the temperature rose slowly and steadily. Corinne moved up and away as the water heated like stew.

She kept her eye on the still-erupting plumes, trying to stay ahead of the hot gray cloud that spewed from them. Her body was slow from the effort of searching. The hot stream billowed out, getting closer and closer to the tip of her tail.

Corinne gathered her strength and surged forward— directly into the path of rows of jagged teeth. She dipped just in time to avoid the mouth of the killer whale, but the body of the creature rolled her, knocking her off her path and making her lose momentum. The gray water caught up to her, searing the tips of her tail. She swam forward again, and the whale slapped her body with its fin, driving her out of its path. She steadied herself and braced for the whale's return attack, but it moved off. Corinne wasn't the killer whale's concern. But in the time she lost, the gray water reached her. It wrapped around her, burning hot. She took off again, but it was everywhere, and she didn't know which way to swim.

A pair of hands pulled Corinne out of the cloud and towed her away, faster than she could move, to clear, cold water.

When they stopped, Corinne drifted just far enough away to see her rescuer was a mer-creature like her, with blue-black skin and scales of silver and black striping his tail. He stared at her with his head tilted. The billowing cloud was dull behind his shining skin and glittering tail, but it wasn't moving any closer to them. A moment later, the cloud slowly dispersed until the water was clear again.

Thank you, Corinne said.

The merman bowed his head. *Wo din de sen?* he asked.

There was something about his voice that sounded familiar, but she couldn't place it, and she didn't know what he was asking.

Who are you? he asked again.

Corinne couldn't remember.

Why are you here? he tried.

She didn't know that either. There had been hot, foggy water, and before that, creatures crawling out of the oddly shaped rocks. Before that, she had been swimming fast, but where she had come from, and where she was headed, she couldn't remember.

The merman touched the necklace at Corinne's neck. She clasped her fingers around it protectively. The grooves of the stone were familiar beneath her fingers.

This is my mama's, she said.

And?

I live on an island.

Yes?

And family should be given a chance to be forgiven.

Understanding spread across the merman's face. *Oh. You are looking for the creature.*

Yes. My aunt, Corinne said. *But how did you know?*

Every creature belongs to another, the merman said. *None of us come from nowhere.*

Is she angry? Corinne asked.

The merman shrugged. *You will have to ask.*

20

The Boys Return

Hugo waited nervously at the front of the bakery all day long. He made bread that came out lopsided, and pies that were charred on the bottom, and he used salt for the glaze instead of sugar.

"They will be back soon," Mrs. Ramdeen said, turning a half-burnt pie in her hands. "They know the mountains like the backs of their hands." She picked off the black bits and handed the rest to Allan, who dove in eagerly. Even on Hugo's worst day, his pastries were delicious.

Hugo nodded, but his chest felt tight. His eyes strained to see out the door and around corners, and inventory every head that jogged down the road.

"They were with the girls," Mrs. Ramdeen assured him. "And if they are back, the boys will be back soon, too."

Hugo thought about Corinne's face when she told him about the boys on the mountain. She had not met his eyes straight on. He swallowed hard.

"Dru has only just come back to the village," Mrs. Ramdeen continued. "She said they had to take a different way down because of all the damage. Then they were a long way off."

Hugo tried to smile. But he knew that the pain in his chest would not go away until his boys returned. He threw out all the baking he had done that afternoon, to the delight of a pack of stray dogs. Then he closed up the pantry and sat with Mrs. Ramdeen on the bench outside. The thin gold bands on Mrs. Ramdeen's wrists clinked together as she patted the baker's hands. The two of them watched Allan draw a ring in the dirt near the side of the road. He took out a bag of marbles and began to pitch the little glass balls against each other. Each tap of the glass and scrape of Allan's foot in the dirt and clink of Mrs. Ramdeen's braceleted hand counted another moment that Bouki and Malik were gone, and another moment that Hugo's heart ached.

He closed his eyes, as if that might make the time move more quickly. The sun beat down on his eyelids. Instead of darkness, he saw pulsing flesh and blood.

"Look!" Allan shouted.

Hugo's eyes flashed open and he stood up so fast that the bench tipped over, knocking Mrs. Ramdeen into the dirt.

Hugo would have picked her up and helped her to dust off, but at the end of the road, just past the market gate, were his boys. He left Allan to help his mother and ran for Bouki and Malik.

The boys seemed bigger to him, as if they had grown overnight. Malik ran into Hugo's outstretched arms. Bouki moved more slowly, but he didn't object to the squeezing hug that Hugo gave them both.

"Are you all right?" he asked.

Malik nodded, his eyes bright, and his smile wide, showing another missing tooth.

"Are you hungry?" he asked.

This time it was Bouki who nodded. "And tired."

"Good, good. Come inside."

Allan and Mrs. Ramdeen smiled at Hugo and the boys. Mrs. Ramdeen patted Hugo on the arm. Hugo caught the tips of her fingers and held them for a second. Then, Mrs. Ramdeen helped Allan put the marbles back into his little pouch, and they made their way up the road.

Hugo fired up the oven and warmed yesterday's bread. He sliced the loaf, grabbed some cheese, and put the food on a plate, which he set with a clatter on the counter in front of the boys. "Now, tell me everything," he said.

"After we got separated, all the usual ways were cut off," Bouki began.

"Yes, yes, I had a feeling. I was so worried."

"But then Malik found a path through the mountain that led all the way to the top." Bouki paused to look at Malik for a moment. His brother was busily chewing and didn't seem to be paying attention. "And we found a village."

"Corinne told me!" Hugo said. "What luck!" He saw Bouki stiffen, and he waited for the next part of the story.

"The people there were helpful," Bouki continued. "They fed us and let us stay the night, and . . ."

Hugo nodded and held his breath.

"And they told us about our parents," Bouki said softly.

Hugo couldn't move, and he couldn't breathe. "Your parents?"

"The village was our home. We forgot it."

Malik looked up at Hugo with a bright smile. "Home!"

Hugo's heart squeezed.

21

A Single Shard

Bouki needed to talk to Corinne. There were things he had learned on the mountain that she would need to know. After they had eaten, he asked Hugo if they could go to the fishing village. Hugo quietly agreed, but when the boys set out on the road, Hugo locked up the bakery and joined them.

The island looked as if a giant hand had picked it up, shaken it, and put it back down again. Everything was out of place—trees, houses, even the animals had wandered far from where they should have been.

In the middle of the road, near the full well, a fat black-and-white cow nosed a pile of leaves. Hugo paused to slap the animal on the rear end. She looked up a moment, then ambled off toward town, hopefully in the direction that would take her home.

The three of them kept going, past the dry well, which was now just a hole in the ground; the stones that once ringed the top had broken off in the storm.

"We have to fill it up," Hugo said. "Someone might fall in."

"On the way back," Bouki insisted. "I need to see Corinne."

Hugo nodded and said nothing else until they came to the house that overlooked the beach, where he called for Pierre.

The house was silent and empty.

Malik tugged at Hugo's white baker's smock and pointed at the beach.

"Of course," he said. "They are probably helping their neighbors below."

But when they passed the lip of the hill, they saw a gathering of people looking out at the waves.

"No," Bouki said softly.

Malik took off running down the hill. Bouki went quickly after him, leaving Hugo to follow behind. The boys pushed their shoulders to part the crowd and made their way to the front. Pierre stood looking out at the glittering sea, his hair flying around his face in the breeze.

"What happened?" Bouki asked.

"She went back," Pierre said. His voice cracked at the end, and nothing else came out to explain.

"Alone?" Bouki asked. "Or was Dru with her?"

"I'm here," Dru said, stepping out of the crowd.

"What about Mama D'Leau?" Bouki asked.

"Corinne went to save her," Dru said. "But she didn't come back."

"She will be back soon," Bouki said, mostly to reassure himself.

Dru shook her head. "Look." She pointed to the horizon, where dark clouds again gathered.

Bouki thrust his hand into his pants pocket until he felt what he was looking for. He walked into the waves. Hugo grabbed him by the collar.

"She will need this, Hugo," he said. "Please."

Hugo shook his head. "No, Bouki."

"Please, Papa."

Hugo let go. Malik moved forward and took Hugo's huge hand in his own small one. Bouki looked away from them and waded through the water until the sea was up to his chest. Then he opened his palm on the surface and let the sea splash into it.

"Come," he said.

On the horizon, water gathered up into a vast pointed wave. It rolled toward them on shore and flattened with the rest of the sea just before it reached Bouki.

"I have something for you," he said. He held his hand up and a small sliver of opal glittered in his fingers.

The surface ruffled and then smoothed. It began to swirl like the water in a drain. Bouki dug his toes into the sand and stood his ground for as long as he could, but the pull of the water got too strong. He closed his fist around the shard of rock as the eddy sucked him under.

22

Tangle in the Water

Corinne followed the merman around the sharp edges of an iceberg. She began to sense the difference in every drop in degree of temperature, in every speck of dust that floated around her, even in the color of the water and the amount of salt she tasted in it.

The currents tugged her in different directions. One twined cold and thin and wrapped around her arm. Another was warmer and brushed the end of her tail. Still another pushed against her body gently, welcoming and less insistent than its sisters. Then there was a fourth that came at her sharp and scraped her skin like the edge of a knife. Each current promised something if only she would take it up on its offer to buoy her somewhere else. She felt the pulse of each one, tasted the water it had to offer. The currents were entire new worlds she could lose herself in. They pressed her, tickled her senses, and bid her to follow them. Something deep within her hungered to go somewhere else, to chase the waves and abandon herself. Corinne could forget her errand. She could leave everything behind. She could follow the currents and the water would lap gently around her forever. It would be so easy. But her heart pounded insistently in her chest. It wanted something, too.

I am Corinne, she said. *Severine is my mother's sister.*

Corinne pushed forward again, breaking the currents' grip on her body. But now that she understood them, she knew where each would lead. She could feel how to use them to move even faster than she had before. She followed the merman more easily now, dipping and rising with the valleys and peaks of the seafloor. All the while, her heart thudded, fearing what would happen when she found her aunt.

It wasn't long before Corinne felt a web-thin pulse. Its pull was weak at first, and then stronger the farther she traveled. Before long the pulse beat in time with her own. The merman had called Severine a creature. She wondered what she would meet. Worried that she might startle Severine, or that the jumbie would not remember who she was, Corinne began to hum, then she added the words she had made up for her aunt months before. She sang.

Hand to hand and heart to heart,
Love can never be torn apart.
Heart to heart and hand to hand,
From water's chill to sun-warmed sand.
Remember Tante siren, doux doux,
Remember waves and grass and sky?
Remember Tante esprit, doux doux,
Remember Corinne, your sister's child?

The pulse of the water quickened, and Corinne's heart leapt, speeding up to match the beat of the waves. She moved more swiftly through the sea, leaving the merman behind and singing her song, until she came to a wide, deep valley with little light. She could feel Severine there, but she couldn't see her, not even with her enhanced jumbie sight. It had come in handy in dark water before, but this darkness felt thick and heavy.

Tante Severine, Corinne called softly.

There was movement in the water. She could feel it tremble, but not from fear. Corinne had learned to sense that. This was something else. Planning. Calculation. She stopped and tried to feel for anything drifting nearby.

The water rippled, reaching out to her like fingers,

and pulled her toward a shallower spot covered by a small cut of ice.

Tante? Corinne said as she moved around the ice floe. She could see better here. Every color brightened in hue. The ice was striped in blue and green, with hints of pink. The water was a kaleidoscope of turquoise and silver and navy shades. But still, she couldn't see her aunt.

The current changed. It gripped her around her middle and drew her in like a line taut with a fish. Corinne tried to wriggle free of its grasp, but it was too strong. The current moved faster, drawing her to a patch of water that was palest green with a tangle of branches at the center. As she came closer, she could see the branches were long and thin and sharp. Corinne was being pulled straight to the tangle. She struggled, trying to save herself from impalement.

Tante! Please! Corinne cried, but the pull didn't slacken or slow.

Corinne shut her eyes, dreading what would come next. She crashed into the branches. Some of the sticks stabbed her skin, others scraped her flesh and scales, another gouged her tail. The branches folded into a cage around her. Her plaits were caught and her arms and tail were trapped. Her skin burned in the places the sticks had cut and bruised. She tasted her own warm blood in the cold water.

Tante, please.

A mouth within the bramble opened. *You will taste nice*, the bramble said. *It's been a while since I've had such a big meal. Only small, small ones of late. A little taste of fin here, a little chunk of tail there. But not a whole, thick thing like you.*

Severine?

Who dat? the bramble snapped.

You, Tante, Corinne said. *We are family. I have come for you.*

The tangle of branches shook. *No, no. Family know each other. Family stick together. Family is not strangers.*

The shaking loosened some of the sticks just enough that Corinne could slip her arm off a branch. She kept it tucked against her chest, clasping her mama's stone to keep it out of Severine's reach. As she moved, a cloud of blood bloomed in the water and the bramble shivered all around her.

Nice, nice! it said, elated. *That blood sweet!*

Corinne heard something like the lapping of a tongue, and the bramble shivered again and giggled.

How I should have you? it asked. *Raw and dripping? Right here in the water? Or should I squeeze you dead and leave you out on the ice to harden for a little crunch?* The bundle tightened, shrinking the cage and pushing the branches further into Corinne's flesh. Corinne shrieked with pain. More blood erupted from her tail. The jumble of twigs rubbed against itself, making a grating sound.

Corinne peered through the snarl and tried to find anything in the water that would help her, but the ocean was empty. Even the merman was nowhere in sight. There wasn't a fish, or plant, or floating object that might be useful.

The twisted bundle pulled Corinne. Corinne felt a current, one that led back to warmer water. She moved her free hand and flexed her fingers, trying to pull at the current. As if it understood, the current came to her. A thin stream wrapped around her little finger. Corinne closed her hand, drawing it in. The water twisted into a small eddy, taking Corinne and Severine with it. It moved them slowly at first, then faster and faster.

What dis? the bramble complained.

Corinne focused on the water. She squeezed her eyes shut and let the current take them, drawing them down to the depths of the sea. It wasn't the current doing this. Corinne was controlling the water, bending it to her will. She could feel the tension between the water droplets that made up the entire ocean; she understood how she could move her fingers and twist the sea around them, moving the currents faster than she could with her own body.

Just before they hit bottom, the current dissipated like clouds after a storm and a new one took them. Corinne's heart beat faster. It was exhilarating, manipulating the water. She played with it, dismissing one current and calling another to pull them toward the surface again.

The tangle loosened enough that Corinne had space to swat against the cage of branches with her tail. The stick that had pierced her went in farther, the jagged edges catching her flesh. She writhed with pain. But to get out she would have to push at the cage of twigs. Corinne slid her tail out again and swatted. The pain was almost unbearable, but with each hit, she loosened the knot around her body.

When she had made a wide-enough hole in the bottom of Severine's cage, she pulled herself down and free of the trap.

Tante, she said, putting a hand to her bleeding arm. *We must leave now.*

You not my family, the knot of branches said.

You are mine, Corinne said. *Come home.*

Corinne called the current around Severine. She needed it to wrap her tightly, and it did. Water swirled around her, holding her branches in place. It must have been what Huracan had done to Mama D'Leau. The tangle of branches shook and tried to escape, but could not.

It sighed. *I didn't even eat yet*, it complained.

There are better things to eat on land, Corinne said.

Like what?

I grow the sweetest oranges on the island, Corinne said.

Juicy, pulpy oranges that taste like sunlight. Come. Corinne reached her hand out. The bramble reached out, too, with long twiggy fingers that stretched and wound around Corinne's hand and up her arm.

Is it far? I don't like to go far.

I will sing to you, then it won't take so long, Corinne said.

The waves of memory crash above us,
Our salty tears wash away.
Mmm Tante, Tante doux doux
Come away, come away, do.

23

Home

Corinne found a strand of water that was warm and sweet. This was the way home, she was sure of it. The sea pulled them back to the island. It dropped off at times, and Corinne had to search to pick it up again. The thicket of twigs at Corinne's side was no help at all. Severine allowed herself to be carried across the vast deep, silent and sullen, like a child who had been scolded.

Every time the current weakened, Severine grew heavier against Corinne's body. The scratching brambles were sharper and more uncomfortable to hold with each loss of momentum and delay.

Stop fidgeting, Corinne snapped.

But it seemed that Severine couldn't help herself.

When the sea began to taste like home, of fleshy mangoes and sharp oranges and milky soursop, the current grew more turbulent. Corinne moved toward the surface, looking forward to trailing her hands through the sargassum leaves that grew in large clumps in the ocean bordering the island. She floated up and took in the wavering reflection of her dark skin, still in her papa's old white shirt. The ripped ends of it trailed alongside the long orange tail that shot out from her lower half and the bramble of wood she pulled along that dug uncomfortably at her sides. But there was no bed of sargassum floating on top of the waves. Instead the sea was littered with rubble. It was as if something had exploded deep in the water and destroyed everything it touched, sending the pieces blackened and broken in every direction. And Corinne tasted something else in the waves: dirt and sweat and blood.

She moved more quickly.

What could do a thing like that? she wondered aloud.

Severine had no explanation.

The current was in chaos now, dropping and pulling every which way, but Corinne didn't need it. Even in total destruction, she knew these waters. She followed the shredded bits of sargassum and broken pieces of coral all the way to the reef. Its usual bright colors and waving fronds were bruised and battered. There were gaping holes in the dense habitat, places where the color looked like it had been drained out, and despite being deep beneath the water, the whole of the coral looked dry and dull, and worse, empty. There were no shrimp or fish darting through and peeking out from gaps. It was a ghost of what it had been.

Corinne turned away from the reef and moved closer to the island then stopped. She needed to think. The same way she had figured out the currents, she was starting to feel the ocean. All of it. Her skin puckered and her pores rose. Every tiny hair on her body was a receptor that read the drops of water like braille. She closed her eyes and let her other senses tell her about the water. It was not only sargassum and bits of coral that disrupted the patterns of the currents. Broken planks of wood, cracked rocks, torn galvanized roofing, and the lifeless bodies of fish, birds, and other animals bumped against each other in the sea. She felt the curve of an overturned boat bending the sea around it. Then she felt something else. Something small, like the body of a person. Her heart quickened and she dashed toward it through the thick rubble and stirred-up sand. Finally she saw it just ahead, a still shape, hidden in the dark behind the layers of water, but her vision cleared as she got closer. Her skin prickled as though she was beginning to sweat and her stomach knotted.

Hey! Severine complained when Corinne gripped her too hard.

Corinne loosened her grip but kept swimming until she was right up on it. She let go of Severine to reach with both hands toward the figure, until she felt it under her palms. It was a hard, cold, stone face and body that she knew.

Bouki.

Something inside Corinne had changed. It wasn't like the strike of a match that suddenly brought light into a room, or the slow glow of a gas lamp as it drew in oil from the wick. It had come on slowly, since the iceberg and the fight with Severine, and maybe even before that. It was a growing sense that she could feel the elements around her, the earth, the water, the air. She could communicate with them in the same way she could with her papa and her friends, with a slight movement of her body, a tiny change in the curve of her mouth. And just as her papa and her friends would come to her aid when she needed it, the elements would help her as well.

All her collected frustration, all her doubt and guilt and worry, erupted from her in one gushing stream.

It blasted from her core and radiated out like an orb. It threw Severine away, vibrated up into the sky, and drilled into the ground. The water rippled, the ground shook, and the sky sizzled. Waves gathered strength and size as they careened outward. As her fury extended, she felt the sea, the sargassum, the sand. She felt the roots of every plant that sucked water and the flesh and blood of every creature that relied on it. For a moment, the world fell silent and still. Even the damp wind and the clouds ceased to move.

Corinne pressed her hand to Bouki's chest. His heart was beating, but his pulse was dim and slow. Corinne closed her eyes and felt through the water again, searching the currents for something large and slithering. Then she darted off, leaving Bouki behind.

Corinne found Mama D'Leau still sitting among the dead, bleached coral even though the current that had trapped her was long broken. The jumbie had her back to Corinne and was curved over something small in her hands, to which she was humming.

Corinne's rage gathered again, like a tightly packed wave, and burst forth against Mama D'Leau's back. The jumbie lurched forward and the thing in her hand fell. It was her opal. She looked back. When she saw Corinne, her eyes narrowed. Corinne pushed the water again, and it rolled toward the jumbie, but this time, Mama D'Leau whipped her tail around, and the force of the water parted and moved to either side of her.

So, Mama D'Leau said.

So, Corinne said.

Corinne raced toward the jumbie, using the water to move even faster. She crashed into Mama D'Leau's stomach with her shoulder, and the jumbie fell back hard on the coral, cracking it. Mama D'Leau pushed herself up.

She moved her hand to her back to assess the damage. Her fingertips were covered in drops of blood, which immediately mixed with the water and disappeared. The jumbie's jaw tightened. Mama D'Leau stared Corinne down and Corinne began to sink. She felt herself grow heavier and heavier. She felt the water being squeezed out of every pore in her skin. Corinne looked down. Her orange tail was turning stone gray.

Corinne fought. She drew water back to herself, absorbing as much of it as she could. She began to feel lighter, until her tail swayed beneath her.

Mama D'Leau's mouth opened in disbelief. She coiled her tail like a spring and launched herself at Corinne. Corinne tried to call the current to push Mama D'Leau away, but it wasn't fast enough. Mama D'Leau was on top of her with her hands around Corinne's neck. She pinned Corinne to the soft golden dirt and squeezed.

As she was pressed farther and farther down, Corinne felt every individual speck of sand, every broken piece of coral, and every torn leaf of seaweed that pressed against her body. She could almost see each of them surrounding her. She could feel the droplets of the water, too, how they were tiny, individual splashes, all moving as one body. She could even sense the air in between all of it, and draw it into her lungs. She let her ability to feel every single thing around her reach out into the sand, across the water, and up into the air. There was the coral reef, the island, the ocean, the heartbeats of people on the surface of both land and sea, every tree and plant and blade of grass rooted to the soil. There was Papa Bois, still as a tree in the forest, and then the rock that was Bouki sunk beneath the waves. She felt the mermaids, the fish, and the leatherback turtles that had come to the island to lay their eggs, but found the shore ravaged and broken.

Corinne's senses reached to other islands, feeling them, tasting them, smelling them, seeing them, hearing them. Then she reached beyond the islands to the oceans, and huge, solid continents. She felt the birds in the sky, and their panic as clouds gathered again, drawing pressure in the air and making it hard for them to keep their equilibrium.

She knew when Mama D'Leau pulled away and backed off toward the dead coral. She knew when Sisi arrived and looked at her with worry in her eyes. But she could also see her father with his feet pointed toward the sea, the muscles in the arc of his heel strained, ready to run to her at any moment. She knew Malik was sitting in the sand at the shore, looking out on the waves for his missing brother. She felt Severine shiver and crawl into a hidden crack in the hill beneath Corinne's home. She couldn't decide what to pay attention to. They were all important, and at the same time, none of them was important.

Sisi picked up Corinne and lifted her to the surface, and took her to the beach, slowly.

Corinne wanted to tell Sisi that she was fine, but she couldn't move or speak. Maybe she had stretched her senses too far. She tried to focus only on the feeling of Sisi's hands under her back, and the swish of her tail in the waves, and the bits of salty sand that drifted into her mouth.

When Sisi reached shore, Pierre, Hugo, Malik, and the entire Duval family were waiting at the edge of the waves. Corinne heard her papa sobbing. She felt Mrs. Duval take her from Sisi, and carry her gently to Pierre. He cradled her in the water. Malik reached out, petted her hair, and then began to cry. Hugo pulled him close. Sisi disappeared and returned moments later, dragging the stone that was Bouki.

Corinne felt for her papa's heartbeat. She felt its regular rhythm and her heart beating in time with his. His warmth washed over her, helping her feel his large, rough hands and the soft nats of his dreadlocked hair against her skin. She felt warmer and warmer, and then cold again as a soft breeze blew past them, puckering her skin.

"Corinne?" Pierre said softly.

"Papa," Corinne said. Corinne reached toward the rock in Sisi's arms and felt until she could sense the heart at the middle of it. She pulled moisture to Bouki's body, softening the stone until his skin went from dull gray to soft reddish brown, starting at the tips of his toes and trailing toward his stomach and chest. Hugo gasped. Mrs.

Duval took Hugo's hand, and they steadied themselves against each other. Laurent's brother Abner whistled softly through a few missing front teeth. In another moment, Bouki quivered in Sisi's arms, warm and safe.

Corinne relaxed and thought about being on land with her papa and her friends, and with the next wash of a wave, her tail was gone.

"How did you do that?" Pierre asked.

Corinne shook her head. She didn't know how to explain.

"Did you find Severine?" Pierre asked.

"You knew where I went?" Corinne asked.

"When you didn't come right back, I knew," Pierre said.

Corinne nodded. She looked up into the darkened sky where the rain was beginning to fall.

"We have to get inside," Pierre said.

Corinne could barely stand, so Pierre picked her up. As he climbed the hill, she asked the sky, "Wasn't it enough? Didn't you get what you wanted?"

The rain came down harder.

"Why wasn't that enough?" She clenched her hands and gritted her teeth.

Pierre put her down and stepped back. "Corinne!"

Corinne looked at her skin. It was red, as if she had been in the sun too long. As raindrops fell on her they sizzled and evaporated. "What's happening?"

Pierre, Hugo, Bouki and Malik, and Laurent and his family were all looking at her, their faces filled with fear. "What's the matter?"

"Corinne," Pierre said again. It was the way he called her on the boat when he wanted her to turn the oar, or pull up the nets, or bail water from the bottom.

"Yes, Papa?"

She saw something in his hands. It was the shirt she had been wearing, and inside of it was her skin, slack in his hands. When Corinne looked down at herself again, she was a bright orange flame against red flesh, hovering just above the ground.

A strong breeze took her higher. She spread her arms, trying to stop herself, but the effort flipped her to the side. She screamed and a tongue of flame burst out, pushing Pierre and the others back.

Raindrops hissed against Corinne's fiery flesh as she floated up and up.

Despite the rain, the entire village emerged from their homes to watch her, bright as a torch, floating into a fist of clouds.

Near the boats, Corinne spotted a beautiful man and woman holding on to each other where the waves met the land, their eyes as wide with concern as the people's of the village. Corinne reached a hand out toward them and flipped again—to face a cloud with the face of a man, angry and waiting.

24

Huracan

The island disappeared behind a gray sheet of rain and clouds, but Corinne felt the bitter rage of Huracan above her. She was electrified. Every part of her crackled with a biting, pinching energy.

The clouds cleared momentarily. Corinne's own island lay below, among the other islands dotting the wider expanse of sea. The green of their lands had been washed out by rain and mud, but embers of fires and gas lamps along the roads traced lines on their backs. People huddled against the rain in the warmth of every shining yellow light, waiting for the hurricane to stop.

Corinne had done all she could to restore balance by

bringing Severine back home. The jumbie that belonged to the land had returned to it, so the jumbie that belonged to the sea would remain in her domain, but it hadn't worked out that way. Then Corinne had nearly lost herself using her newfound power. What would happen if she tried to use that power again? She might never come back.

Corinne floated above the rain clouds to drier air that didn't sizzle against her skin. Above her, the sky was a deep blue and stars were just appearing in dots of silver that mirrored the yellow flickers on each island. But the starlight was cold and silent.

The air thinned. Corinne struggled to breathe. The cold closed in around her throat and her fire paled to yellow. As the last threads of heat slipped from her body, Corinne heard a deep, gruff voice: "You have done enough. No more."

It wasn't true. She thought she had done enough, but it wasn't. She hadn't helped anyone. Not herself, not her papa, not her friends, no one.

A defiant fire radiated from Corinne's body. The flames around her strengthened and leapt away in a burst of orange. She shimmered against the blue of the night.

Wisps of cloud assembled around her.

"Huracan," Corinne said.

"Who are you to challenge me?" the voice boomed. It came from every direction at once, as if Corinne was inside the god's throat.

Corinne tried to say her own name, but the cold closed in and she couldn't find her voice. She focused on the air against her skin and felt a small pocket of thinner pressure to her left. She strained toward it and her body drifted into the space. She was out of the cloud. Next to her, thick and thin wisps formed into the face of a man. He was young-looking, with straight hair that fell to his shoulders, a wide, flat nose, and thin lips curled into a snarl, which turned slack with surprise when Corinne wasn't where he thought she would be. The face disappeared. Corinne felt for the air current again, turning when it turned, trying to see Huracan form again, but he was mist and she had no hope of keeping up. She stayed still.

Lightning crackled the air around her; electricity popped against her skin like newly bursting flames. She shrieked and spewed more fire. The clouds parted in the path of her cry.

Corinne turned and tried to summon her strength again. Where Huracan had reassembled she tried to breathe fire. Nothing but hot air came out. Again, Huracan disappeared. For a moment, Corinne thought she saw a small curving line in the mist, like a smirk without a face.

The clouds pulled away and Corinne was able to breathe more easily. "What do you want?" she asked.

"I want peace," Huracan said, rumbling like thunder.

"You're destroying people's homes. That isn't peace," Corinne said.

< 177 >

"Peace is quiet," Huracan said. "Peace is still. Better to wipe out everything and start again fresh."

A thick patch of clouds formed into the shape of a man walking with his hands behind his back, one leg a fishtail that flapped with every step.

Corinne felt for the fire in her core again and huffed at the god. A thin, yellow flame erupted from her, but before it reached Huracan, he dissolved into a thin mist and was gone.

Corinne turned—and came face-to-face with the god, whose head was now the size of her whole body.

"You're killing us," she said.

"So what?"

"I know this is my fault," Corinne said. "I can fix it. Just tell me how."

"You can fix this? Who do you think you are?"

"I'm Corinne. Corinne La Mer."

"Nicole's child."

"You knew my mother?"

The mist seemed to be looking at her more carefully. "Yes, I knew her."

"My papa said that she died in a hurricane." Corinne found the pocket of air pressure more easily now. She shifted into it to come closer to Huracan's face. "A hurricane with lightning. Was that you?"

Huracan re-formed more solidly into a man and stood

before Corinne. "What can wind do but blow? What can rain do but fall? I do what I have to do. I can't control who gets hurt."

Corinne's heart constricted. She sank lower in the sky. "You killed my mother."

"When your papa fishes in the sea, does he choose which fish live and which die in his nets?" Huracan asked.

"That's not the same thing," Corinne said.

"No?" Huracan said. "Life is life and death is death." The clouds re-formed into a cold, calculating face with eyes that glittered from the stars behind them.

"But these storms," Corinne said. "You mean to kill us all?"

Lightning crackled across the sky again, and Corinne shrieked in pain. The god rumbled his reply in the thunder that followed. "Yes. All."

Corinne hurtled to earth. Her flames extinguished and every particle of air burned her raw, exposed body as she fell. She hit the beach hard, sending sand in every direction.

Corinne screamed. The combination of the fall and the sea salt against her raw skin ravaged her. She tried not to move.

The rain had stopped. From where Corinne lay still, she saw the shape of Marlene's tiny body running toward her in the darkness. The girl carried a calabash gourd, large enough that she needed both hands to hold it. Her steps faltered a moment and her eyes went huge when she saw Corinne, but she kept coming. At last, she held the calabash out low. Inside it was a pile of something velvety and brown. Corinne touched it and felt her skin fold back around her.

Behind Marlene, nearly the entire village came running, with Pierre leading them. Corinne had never felt more exhausted. She could barely move and it was hard to breathe. She managed to whisper her thanks to Marlene as she lay in the wet sand with the waves kissing her feet.

"We can't stay here," Corinne said. Above her, a tangle of clouds formed with silver lightning that shot through it like veins. "We have to get everyone away."

"There is nowhere to go," Victor argued. Corinne caught a glimpse of him, wet and stiff with anger. "That is your own fault."

"This is not the girl's fault," Mrs. Duval said. "She has done everything to try to help us."

Corinne tried to turn her head toward Mrs. Duval to thank her, but the pain of that small movement throbbed inside her skull. She closed her eyes and opened them again, struggling to focus. Behind Victor, Corinne noticed the beautiful man and woman she had seen before on the beach. She seemed to be the only one who recognized who they really were.

Pierre and Mrs. Duval helped Corinne up.

"Where do we go?" Mrs. Duval asked.

"Back to the mountains," Corinne said. "It was the safest place."

As the crowd scattered, murmuring about the essentials they would collect for the trip, Mama D'Leau came to Corinne, walking gracefully in her human form. She wore the garb of the women of the island, a crisp white blouse that opened to show her dark shoulders, a colorful skirt, and a head tie wrapped around her hair and piled high to accommodate her voluminous braids. "I didn't mean to hurt you so," she said.

"And what about Bouki?" Corinne asked.

The jumbie stiffened. It was true she had hurt the boy. He had wrecked her stone and diminished her power. "He had something of mine. He tricked me."

Corinne wanted to laugh, but her chest burned. Whatever Bouki had done, he had managed to get away with it. "He would be the only one who could." She beckoned Mama D'Leau and Papa Bois to come closer. "It didn't work. Bringing Severine back wasn't enough," she said.

Papa Bois put his hands into the pockets of his dark pants. His short-sleeved shirt ruffled in the breeze. He bowed his head and glanced at Mama D'Leau.

"What now?" Corinne asked. "What exactly did Bouki do to trick you?"

"When he returned the stone to me it was broken," Mama D'Leau explained.

"It wasn't," Corinne said.

"Not when you had it," she said. "He did that himself, but he told me it was damaged when you fled Ma Dessaly and her sons."

"And with the stone damaged . . ." Corinne began.

"I am not quite myself," said Mama D'Leau. "There is only so much I can do." She reached into her headwrap and pulled out the opal. It shimmered in her hands. As she turned it, the sliver slipped out of its crack and she pushed it back in.

Papa Bois squeezed her hand gently. "We have survived his storms before. We will survive again," he said.

"You have. What about the rest of us?" Corinne squinted at the jumbies as they looked at each other. "There is something you can do, isn't there?" Corinne asked. "Please. We have to try everything."

"You right. It always have another way."

"Huracan said he could only be himself," Corinne said, frowning. "We must be ourselves—our true selves—too."

Mama D'Leau sighed. "He will tire of these storms, you know. He can't blow forever."

Corinne bit her lip. "I will do everything I can," she said, looking at Papa Bois. "You said that you can't go into the sky? Well, now I can."

"He will kill you, Corinne."

"Not if you help me," she pleaded. "Both of you. We can do this if we do it all together."

Mama D'Leau closed her eyes and set her jaw. "I don't have the strength."

"Then I will do what I can alone."

25

The Belly of the Mountain

The people of the villages moved achingly slow, as if every droplet of rain was pushing them farther into the mud.

Corinne followed toward the back of the line. When they went past the bakery, she knocked softly. Hugo opened the top of the Dutch door and looked out, a gas lamp in his hand. At the sight of Corinne's and Pierre's faces, he didn't hesitate. He called the boys, and they all fell in line with Corinne's neighbors from the fishing village and all the other people they had picked up along the way.

The boys pushed to the front and led the way.

The going was unsteady and dangerous in the dark.

Paths and traces had been cut off by mud and rock slides. Rivulets flowed in places that had been dry land, quick and strong despite their small size. Handheld gas lamps, empty of fuel or doused by the rain, flickered out. Some broke when their owners slipped on the slick ground, leaving shards of glass on the already tricky paths. Fat fish lay with their mouths open among the rocks, far from any water. A large cow was on its side, as three *corbeaus* pecked at its bloated stomach. Most of the crowd averted their eyes from the corbeaus' meal. At least the rain didn't begin again until they reached the other side, in the shadow of the mountain, where the brunt of the storm fell against its great stone back.

The landscape was totally different. The path they had taken the day before was cut off by several fallen trees.

Bouki lifted his lantern, looking for a way forward, then turned back to the crowd and shook his head.

Malik tugged his brother's shirt and made a curve with his hand, pointing around the mountain.

"There is another way," Bouki announced. "But it is not easy."

There was grumbling in the crowd, but Hugo fell into step behind the boys and everyone followed. The rain came down harder. Mud covered everything: the path, the trees, the people—even their lanterns were splattered with it. The going was slower than the last time. The ground, ravaged by the first two storms, was like an open mouth of sharp, broken teeth. Not one person escaped without a cut or bruise.

When they reached the place where Malik had found the slit in the rocks, fallen trees and rocks had changed the face of the wall, making it unfamiliar. They felt their way around until Malik's arm slipped through.

The entrance seemed even thinner than it had before. Hugo moved to the front and put his shoulder against one of the boulders, while Pierre and Victor heaved at the other side. They grunted and pushed until the rocks gave way, widening the path just enough for one person to squeeze through at a time.

Bouki held his lamp high as he ushered everyone into the belly of the mountain. In the darkness, dozens of gas lamps bobbed and swayed, illuminating frightened faces as people tripped over stalagmites and worried about stalactites that hung dangerously over their heads. All around them thunder boomed and shook the mountain to its core, making the red mud drawings of hunters throwing spears into beasts tremble, in what seemed like a warning.

From ahead of Corinne came the noise of a scuffle. Corinne found Dru and her family in the crowd and together they pressed forward to find out what was going on.

Victor was standing in the way of a couple, his fists tight and ready. "You think I don't know who you are?" he asked them. He moved one hand to the fisherman's knife looped into the waist of his pants and drew it partway out of its leather sheath. It was sharp enough to cut tangled nets, or to gut a fish in one slice. Even in the low light, its edge gleamed like a stroke of lightning. "Do you want to tell these people the truth? Or should I?"

"It's Mama D'Leau and Papa Bois," Corinne whispered to Dru.

"What are they doing here?" Dru asked. "I didn't think she could get so far from the water."

"They are hiding," Corinne said. "Even they can't stand up against Huracan."

"I asked you a question," Victor demanded.

"Victor." Pierre held up his hands. "This is not the time. We need to get everyone to safety."

"We will never be safe with jumbies among us," Victor said loudly.

There were gasps from the crowd, and then everyone hushed. The only sounds were the wind howling on the other side of the rocks and the drip of water from the cave ceiling to the rocky floor below.

Papa Bois tried to sidestep Victor, but the fisherman caught his arm and shoved him to the floor. Papa Bois's skin turned sallow and wrinkles creased around his eyes. Gray hair threaded through his dark braids.

Victor's eyes were wide. "You see?" he called out. His voice echoed on the walls and rung through the mountain.

Mama D'Leau ran to Papa Bois and pulled him up. Papa Bois's body returned to that of a strong young man.

Victor wheeled in the crowd. "So who else here is a jumbie?" he asked. "And when are you going to turn?" He moved to a man so tall he had to duck beneath a stalactite to stand in the cave. He had a thick beard and hairy arms. "And what happens to the rest of us when you do?" He stared at the man, but the man simply blinked back at him.

"You are frightened, Victor," said Miss Aileen, the eddoes seller who sat near Corinne at the market.

"I'm not afraid." Victor pointed at Mama D'Leau and Papa Bois. "I'm not wrong about them, or about you either." A few people in the crowd shuffled into place behind Victor. He puffed out his chest. "I am not the only one who feels this way."

Pierre put himself in front of Corinne. "We have to get through this together," he said. "No one is forcing you to be here, but leaving now is too dangerous."

"You think they should stay with us?" Victor asked.

"I think we are all better together," Pierre said.

"Oho!" Victor backed off as he fingered the knife at his waist. "Let's see how many of you survive." He moved down the path. "You are all fools."

"Stay with us, it's safer," Pierre said.

Victor shook his head. "It will never be safe with them." He used his lips to point at the tall, hairy man and continued moving away, alone, until he disappeared in the darkness.

Pierre stared at the people who had backed Victor.

They looked everywhere else. "They are all afraid, like Miss Aileen said," Pierre explained as he rubbed Corinne's arm.

"The rest of us are afraid, too," Dru said. "We're all trying to be safe. The jumbies aren't any different."

Pierre found Mr. and Mrs. Rootsingh's eyes in the crowd and smiled at them. "Just so, eh?"

With Victor gone, the group returned to trudging up the mountain. At the top, where the cave was supposed to be, only a small opening remained. The mouth had collapsed shut.

"We're stuck?" Dru asked.

Bouki picked up a pebble and tossed it through the opening. He listened to it clatter on the ground. "The cave is open on the other side of this," he said.

"We can move the rocks," Hugo said.

"No," Pierre said. He pointed up at the ceiling. There were long cracks running through the stones, from which dust fell in thin cascades. "The whole thing could come down on our heads."

"We can wait it out inside the mountain," Corinne suggested.

Malik shook his head.

"It's going to be uncomfortable," Bouki said. "There isn't much space to sit here, and nobody brought enough supplies. Lower down, we were close enough to the river, but up here there's nothing."

"I'm already thirsty," Corinne said.

Malik held up his lamp. It was nearly out of oil, and the light had dipped to a low blue flame.

"That too," Dru said.

"We have no choice but to wait," Pierre said.

Corinne looked around the crowd and frowned. "Papa Bois?" she called. The jumbie stepped forward. In form he was still a young man, and tall, and dark as coal, nearly the same color as the long hair that fell to his waist. It was amazing how good he was at hiding in plain sight. "Can you take us through?"

"To where?" he asked.

"To the village," Corinne said. "Straight up."

Another peal of thunder rolled through, sending shockwaves through the stone. Everyone looked at the cracked ceiling of the cave.

"Will they take us?" Pierre asked. "It was only you four the last time."

"There's nowhere else to go," Corinne said.

"We should still ask," Mrs. Rootsingh said.

"What if they refuse?" asked Miss Aileen.

"They won't," Bouki said.

"Quickly, Papa Bois," Dru said.

"Drupatee!" Mrs. Rootsingh snapped.

"Please," Dru added hastily.

"She is right," Papa Bois said. "I'm not known for speed, but I will try." He squeezed Mama D'Leau's fingers a long moment, then removed his hand from hers.

"You can't," Mama D'Leau said. She stood taller than he was. Her skirt, in hues of deep blue, folded and smoothed like the surface of water as she moved. "Transporting so many will drain you."

"We must help, *cherie*," he said. "We will do it together." He reached for her, but she shook her head and kept her arms to her side. It was the second time Corinne saw worry crease her face.

Papa Bois stepped away. With each step he became more jumbie. His toes curled in under his feet and became small, hard hooves. The black of his hair threaded with gray and lightened to a frost. Two small horns pushed through the thicket of braids on top of his head. He hunched forward and from out of nowhere pulled a stick to lean against. In the flickering light of the dimming lamps, he stood before the crowd, small and ancient.

"He looks different," Dru whispered to Corinne.

"He's . . . weaker." Corinne was surprised, too.

"But why?" Dru asked.

Corinne looked at Mama D'Leau. She also looked weaker. She didn't stand as tall as she had before, but she still appeared to be human, a woman with long legs who held her head proudly. "I don't know," Corinne said. "I've never seen one of them as a jumbie while the other remained human. They always change together."

"Maybe they don't have to," Dru said.

"Especially since she has some extra help," Corinne said.

"Like what?"

"The opal."

Papa Bois leaned heavily against his walking stick. "I can take all of you through the rocks."

A murmur of questions went through the crowd.

Papa Bois reached a hand out, but no one moved forward to take it.

"I'll show you," Corinne said. "He can take me first."

"I'll come too," Pierre said quickly.

The two of them clasped hands with Papa Bois. "It's better if you hold your breath," the jumbie said.

As soon as Corinne inhaled, she felt her body pushing against the rocks, and then through them. It was instantly cooler in the cave than it had been in the narrow passage filled with people, but Corinne had the eerie sensation of being in too close a space. Soon Corinne and Pierre emerged in that cup of mountain where the village stood. As soon as she felt fresh air on her face she opened her eyes. Her head was just above the wet grass. She and Pierre bloomed from the ground, slowly and smoothly into heavy rain. When they were completely through, Papa Bois staggered a little, and Pierre caught him by the arm.

"Are you sure you can do this?" he asked.

Papa Bois nodded.

A flash of lightning illuminated the mountain's highest peak. Huracan was not giving up. The people could hide inside the rocks, or on top of it, but the god wasn't going to stop until something made him.

"I'll go back," Pierre said. "I'll be able to convince everyone to come along." He placed a firm hand on Corinne's shoulder and looked into the village. "Be polite when you let them know what's happening."

"Yes, Papa," she said. She turned to Papa Bois. "Remember what I asked you?"

"That will not be easy," the jumbie said.

"We can only try," said Corinne.

Pierre and Papa Bois sank into the wet grass and disappeared as silently as they had come.

A lamp came on in the village, and the wide frame of Aunty Lu emerged from one of the houses. "Corinne?" she asked. "What are you doing here?"

"When the storm started again, everyone went to the mountains, but the way to the caves was cut off." She took a breath. "We need a place to stay. Please."

Aunty Lu nodded quickly. "We will work it out." People began to grow through the wet grass near them. There was Dru's family, Mrs. Duval and her children, and Marlene and Mrs. Chow.

"But what is this?" Aunty Lu cried, hop-stepping out of the way of the heads that were popping up like flowers from the ground.

"There are more coming," Corinne said, as the first group emerged all the way to their feet.

"Come. Follow me." Aunty Lu hurried toward the village, beckoning everyone with her.

Corinne turned toward the mountain's peak. At its top, she could be close to Huracan. Then, if Papa Bois and Mama D'Leau did their part, too, she might be able to help. As soon as she started toward the mountain, a bolt of lightning hit it, exploding rocks into the air. Corinne saw a hand in the lightning flash. It was a warning. She stopped.

The rocks hurtled back to earth. "Run!" Aunty Lu yelled.

Most everyone went toward the village, but Corinne ran to the passageway that would lead to the mountain's peak. She dodged the rocks raining down on her as she went, as well as the ones rolling on the ground across her path. When she reached the passageway, she looked back. Papa Bois was still standing in the grass, calmly facing the stones bounding toward him. He leaned lightly on his stick as the avalanche slowed and then stopped, with the largest rock coming to rest at his hooves.

Papa Bois turned his face to the sky and seethed. Corinne was sure he was looking into the god's face. Then he turned and nodded once at Corinne.

26

A Plan in Motion

The boys stood with Mama D'Leau, Pierre, and Hugo as Papa Bois ferried people through the rocks. After four trips there was only one small group remaining.

There was another roll of thunder above their heads, and then the sound of crashing. The mountain shook around them and the cracks overhead widened, showering pebbles and dust on their heads.

"Is it me, or is it getting worse?" Hugo whispered.

"We need to move," Bouki said.

Papa Bois reemerged from the rocks looking grayer and smaller than he had when he began.

Mama D'Leau hung back. "Yuh will kill yuhself," she said.

Papa Bois reached a hand toward her. The veins in his arms stood out, as if he had strained every muscle to its maximum. "Come," he said. "She will need us."

"Are you talking about Corinne?" Pierre asked.

Papa Bois bowed his head. "Nothing has happened, La Mer," he said. "But we must all stick together and do what we are best at."

"I will not go," Mama D'Leau said.

Malik moved to her and folded his fingers into hers.

"Don't 'fraid," Papa Bois said gently. He took her other hand and turned to the others. "Remember to—"

"Hold your breath," Miss Aileen finished. "You've said it every time," she added, smiling.

Papa Bois steadied himself against his walking stick and his eyes steeled. The entire group moved into the rock wall. Last of them was Mama D'Leau, whose face screwed up with horror as she was pulled inside the rocks.

They reappeared on the surface with the rain pounding them from all sides. Lightning struck the mountain like a hammer, shaking the ground around them.

Pierre and Hugo grabbed the boys and ran to the village, tripping over the field of rocks from the last blast. Aunty Lu met them at the first set of houses. Malik reached toward her, out of Hugo's arms. She smiled at Hugo, but he didn't return it. She led them to a large, central building, the same one the children had eaten in the day before with the doors at cardinal points. There was another boom and the entire room shuddered. A series of rumbling crashes followed.

The last two to the building were Mama D'Leau and Papa Bois. They leaned against each other, with Mama D'Leau carrying most of Papa Bois's weight. His eyes were closed, but his hooves still moved on their own.

Dru and the boys met them at the south door.

"How is he?" she asked.

"He not going to make it," Mama D'Leau said.

"I will make it," Papa Bois whispered. "If you do your part."

Mama D'Leau stiffened. "I go a long way to get what I want," she said. "Why I should give that up now?"

Thunder ripped across the sky, and everyone ducked and covered their ears at the sound. "You must," Papa Bois said.

"If we leave each other now . . ." Mama D'Leau whispered.

"There is no choice," Papa Bois said. He tried to move away from Mama D'Leau and stand on his own feet. Malik spotted a shadow looming in the doorway. He moved to intercept, but it was too late.

Victor charged into Papa Bois's side, knocking him to the floor and toppling Mama D'Leau with him.

"It's your kind that caused all this," Victor said. He was

soaked to the skin and breathed hard, as if he had taken a difficult climb.

"They are helping us," Dru said.

"Cause a problem just to fix it?" Victor said with a laugh. He got to his feet and wiped spittle from his mouth.

Dru walked up to him. "Didn't you run off? Maybe you should keep running." Her eyes widened, as if she was surprised at her own words. She looked for her mother in the crowd. Mrs. Rootsingh cocked an eyebrow and nodded firmly. Dru turned to Victor again. "Back off!"

Malik stood at Dru's side, and Bouki came up next to him.

Victor's eyebrows rose, but his jaw was a hard line. He took a step back and lowered his head like a bull about to charge. He narrowed his eyes. "Get out of the way. You don't know what you're doing." He swiped the three of them aside, pushing them into Papa Bois as the jumbie tried to pick himself up.

Papa Bois stumbled backward. Mama D'Leau caught him, but her head tie came undone in the scuffle. It unraveled, along with her braided hair, spilling to the floor. Her opal rolled out with her unfurling hair and fell to the ground. It wobbled out of the cloth and shone like a huge drop of water that contained bits of coral and seaweed.

Mama D'Leau gasped and reached for it as Victor's eyes became cruel and his mouth widened with pleasure. They both scrambled for the stone, but Malik dove under them, trying to cover it with his body. Before he got to it, Mama D'Leau knocked it out of the way, and the stone skidded into the crowd, bounding off someone's foot and spinning into the shadows.

Mama D'Leau dropped to her knees. Victor shoved his way through people. Bouki and Dru went after Victor, but Malik turned when he heard a soft thud behind him.

Mama D'Leau writhed in anguish as her legs fused and became scaly under her skirt, and her body lengthened.

Papa Bois reached for Mama D'Leau, but she turned away, shielding her face with her hands. He moved more slowly and scooped her up in his arms. His stick fell away and he tried to steady himself on his goat's legs.

Malik tapped Papa Bois's leg and looked up at him.

"She has to get into the rain," Papa Bois said.

Pierre and Hugo turned to help the jumbies.

"The opal," Mama D'Leau cried. "You must get it."

"You have to let it go, love," Papa Bois said.

"Just that," she said. "*I* have to be the one to let it go. Otherwise is all for nothing."

As Pierre and Hugo took Mama D'Leau's lengthening, undulating body out of the building, Malik looked back and found Victor in the crowd.

27

Determination

Corinne had the feeling she was being followed, but she couldn't stop. She couldn't even turn and look. There was no time. Every lightning strike hit the mountain now, shaking loose larger and larger rocks. Each time, Corinne pressed against the side of the mountain for protection, but the rocks still hit her. Larger ones left bruises that made each of Corinne's movements ache. Sharper ones left scratches that burned in the rain. But Huracan wouldn't stop, so neither would she.

28

Race for the Stone

D ru tracked Victor through the crowd, watching as he pushed, shoved, and stepped on anyone in his way. His head moved in every direction, his gaze scanning the ground. He hadn't spotted the opal yet. The boys were also searching. They had him outnumbered. It was Dru's only relief.

She hopped over bodies and crawled under limbs, hoping to catch a glimpse of the rock before Victor did. She was to his right when she heard him grunt with satisfaction and her heart sank.

Victor bent down and Dru hurtled herself at him.

She knocked him off his feet and sent him crashing into Malik, who groaned under the fisherman's weight.

< 201 >

"Don't let him go!" Dru shouted.

Malik wrapped his legs around Victor's arm and his little hands around his head.

"Get off!" Victor growled.

"You get off my brother!" Bouki hollered.

Dru spotted the stone, shining like the sea. She got to her knees and crawled to it, grabbing it just as Victor caught her ankles and dragged her across the floor.

"Let go of my child!" Mrs. Rootsingh slapped Victor across the face and Bouki charged into Victor's side.

"What are you doing to these children?" Aunty Lu cried, coming up behind Victor and hemming him in between herself and Mrs. Rootsingh.

"She is going to help that jumbie," Victor said. "I don't want to hurt your child. I want to stop *her* from helping the jumbie that's hurting us all."

"Which jumbie is that?" Mrs. Rootsingh asked. "The one who helped get everyone to safety up here in this village?"

"The one who saved all the children from the lagoon?" Mrs. Chow piped up.

"What did that jumbie do to you?" Aunty Lu asked.

Victor tried to back away, but there was nowhere for him to go. Everyone glared at him, waiting for an answer.

Then Mrs. Chow dropped her eyes and looked around her. She turned pale. "Where is Marlene?"

29

A Little Help

The peak of the mountain had been blasted into a flat surface covered in grayish mud. Corinne scrambled to the top. The ground beneath her was still warm from the last lightning strike. She felt its energy surging up through her feet and all through her body.

Now all she needed to do was turn.

And rise up to Huracan.

And stop him.

Fear muted every sensation as one word consumed her: *how.*

"Do you need help?" a small voice asked.

Marlene stood near the edge, the blue ribbon in her hair plastered to her head from the rain. She held her hands behind her back, clearly hiding something from Corinne.

"Marlene! You could have gotten hurt."

"You too, Corinne," she said, frowning. She looked down the side. "I'm a good climber."

"It isn't safe here. You need to go back," Corinne said.

"But you need help," Marlene insisted. She grinned and pulled her hands to the front. In them was the large calabash. "Who will take care of your skin?"

Corinne sighed.

"Go on." Marlene turned her head to the side and squeezed her eyes shut. "Take it off." Then she opened one eye to peek.

"I don't know how," Corinne admitted.

Marlene's hands dropped. She turned the calabash in her fingers. "How did it happen before?" she asked.

"I don't know how," Corinne said. "I was just angry, and then it happened."

"You're not angry anymore?" Marlene asked.

"Yes! I am!"

"Okay, then," Marlene said. She held the calabash out. "Go on."

30

The Last Goodbye

Papa Bois knelt in the mud as Hugo and Pierre laid Mama D'Leau in the wet grass. The rain seemed to soothe her, and her tail continued to extend outward, growing longer and larger as they stepped away. She moaned in pain.

"It never hurt her to turn before," Dru said. "Not when I saw it happen."

"She has been human too long this time," Papa Bois said. "It weakens us. It is easier when we do it together. But alone . . ." He shook his head.

"What do you mean?" Dru asked.

"We made a choice to become human together, so

we could be forever close. But I had to turn back without her. My leaving her had consequences. We knew that. She wanted me to stay with her. Now, she suffers. Because of me."

"Can't you both just turn back?" Dru asked.

"Only once more," the jumbie said. "Then never again."

Dru handed the stone to him.

Papa Bois took the stone to Mama D'Leau as she lay in the grass, her tail flicking in the mud. "Look, cherie," he said.

Mama D'Leau wrapped her fingers around the stone and Papa Bois's fingers. She seemed to relax. "*Merci*," she replied. "So is time, then?"

"*Oui*," Papa Bois said.

Mama D'Leau moved her tail under her and got upright. Then the two of them went to the edge of the village, to the cliff.

Dru followed with Pierre and Hugo. Each put a hand on Dru's shoulder as they neared the ledge. Lightning flashed and Dru saw the same water, black with pitch, that she and Corinne had splashed into when they took the basket down the side of the mountain.

Papa Bois wrapped his hands around Mama D'Leau's with the opal safe inside her palms.

"What if it doesn't work?" she asked.

Papa Bois smiled. "Have confidence, cherie."

Mama D'Leau straightened her body. "Together?"

"Together," Papa Bois said.

They pulled back and threw the opal into the air. It flipped end on end, wobbling slightly, and then arced down and disappeared in the darkness.

"Let the pitch keep it," Papa Bois said.

"Maybe another time, we could—" Mama D'Leau began.

"Maybe." Papa Bois held Mama D'Leau in his arms for a moment. "You understand what she meant?" he asked.

"About being we true selves?" She took a deep breath. "Yes."

"She is a smart girl."

"The witch was right about her," Mama D'Leau said. "She go fix this whole mess." The jumbie pulled away. Her copper body and glistening tail shone in the lightning. She moved even closer to the edge, coiling her tail underneath her. Then she sprang backward with her tail whipping after her, hurtling in an arc down to the black water below.

31

The Fire Within

Marlene opened her other eye and turned to Corinne. "Well?"

"Maybe I'm not angry enough," Corinne said.

"What were you angry about before?" Marlene asked.

"I was mad because I had tried everything to help and nothing did. I was mad because Severine hurt me. It still hurts now." Corinne rubbed a dark bruise on her arm. "I was mad that I knew anything about jumbies at all, which wouldn't have happened in the first place if Bouki and Malik didn't tie my mama's necklace to an agouti!" Corinne held the leather-wrapped stone at her neck. "I was mad that I hurt my papa. I was mad that my friends were taken and hidden underwater and I had to make a bargain with Mama D'Leau to save them. I was mad that people still look at me as if I'm something to fear. I was mad because I was tired." She took a deep breath. "I was mad at everything!"

Marlene bit her lip and set the calabash down. She came to Corinne and hugged her. Then she looked into the sky, shielding her eyes from the rain with the palm of her hand. "The lightning stopped," she said.

Corinne looked up too. "It did."

"How come?" Marlene asked.

"Even Huracan knows I'm not a threat," Corinne said, wiping her eyes and nose with the back of her hand.

Marlene got to her feet and grabbed a handful of rocks, pelting them into the air. "Stupid god!" she screamed. "Dumb, stinky, mean god!"

"Marlene!"

"What?"

The sky darkened just above them as if the clouds had suddenly become thicker.

"Marlene," Corinne said again. The girls grabbed each other's hands and backed away, but they soon came to the edge of the plateau that had been blasted out of the peak. The thicket of clouds grew larger and closer. Light flickered within it, like something striking a match, and a thin thread of lightning shot out from the center, arcing straight toward the girls. They dove to the ground, letting go of each other's hands, and the lightning missed its mark, striking the ground near Marlene's feet, sending up a spray of rocks and mud.

Marlene gasped and stumbled backward. Corinne reached to catch Marlene before she fell over the edge. The little girl's eyes widened, and then she grinned. The hand Corinne reached out was pure fire.

32

Let We See

The sulfur water of the pitch lake soothed the last aches in Mama D'Leau's body the moment she splashed down. She sensed the opal sinking into the thick pitch, being swallowed in its depths. In all likelihood she would never find her stone again, but never was a real long time, eh? Who was to say?

Mama D'Leau had other things to do, though. It was too dark to see, so she tasted the water to find what she needed—a disturbance in the flow, where one current strained against all the rest. It wasn't hard to find. She put all her energy into reaching it, and as she swam, she laughed.

You think you can hold me hostage in mih own water? she said. *Well, let we see now.*

33

A Place to Hide

The tiny, scuttling thing that looked like a tangle of branches had followed along in the trail of people as they fled for the mountains. She had fitted herself inside any crack and crevice, bending and folding and making herself as small as she could to hide, but the tide kept rising, and water seeped everywhere. Bolts of lightning cracked the ground and thunder roared in the sky.

Nowhere was safe for a thing as brittle as she was.

Severine sniffed the ground and found the weak odor of her sister's child, nearly washed away by the rain. She traced the child's scent to the mountain and felt the firmness of the rocks under her twig-thin fingers.

Here was a place to hide, a place that could protect.

Another bolt of lightning hit the top and exploded. Rocks came tumbling down the sides, and Severine's twig body pressed up against the wall of the mountain like a stack of branches, waiting for the shaking to stop. It was a while before the rocks reached all the way to where she was, but when they did, they hurtled against her thin body and ripped away something that cracked like bone and wood.

Severine cried out, but the booming blast of thunder covered the sound.

34

Cloud Fight

Corinne pulled Marlene to safety and turned toward the sky. She burst through a cloud thick with rain, hovering just above it. She wanted to call out, but didn't quite know what to say. Instead, she waited.

She felt the air pressure change from a loose breeze to her left, to something denser and more pressing. She turned to face it.

A gust of wind exploded against her body and pushed her away, sending her spinning into the wet darkness. She righted herself and concentrated. The air was gathering again, this time at her back. Before it came to its full strength, she shot upward and the gust caught only her leg, tossing her foot over head like a pinwheel. She used another pocket of air to pull herself to a stop and lowered herself gently, finding a spot of thick, wet cloud to rest.

Wherever she went, the mist around her evaporated, burned away by her fire.

The air pressure mounted again, squeezing her like pincers. Her fire sputtered. She flattened her body and slipped out of its grasp, sliding along the misty top of a cloud, boiling it away as she went. Just as quickly, the cloud thickened again as if she had not caused any harm to it at all.

Corinne closed her eyes and tried to sense Huracan himself, not just the blows he dealt. Once again, the air pressure gathered, but lightning crackled beneath it.

Corinne's eyes flashed open as the light sparked just beneath her body. She hurtled herself to the right. The lightning shot out, reaching like thin, gnarled fingers, each one trying to catch her on the sharp edge of its nail.

The air electrified and popped against her flesh, throwing every nerve into anguish. The popping stopped and a cold gust chilled her to the bone. She dropped several feet until a cushion of air buoyed her back up. She could almost see the cloud tightening above her, almost feel the knuckle of it readying to take another swing. She shifted her weight to another, lighter current that would take her away from Huracan's fist.

The strike blew past Corinne, but the cold wind it drew

cut against her raw skin and nearly put out her flame. The chill numbed her senses, stupefying her long enough for Huracan to land a blow. Corinne was knocked back and vibrated heat until Huracan's mist burned away, forming a black hole in the center of his fist.

Thunder gargled with anger all around her. She covered her ears, but hated the sound of her own raw, wet, squelching body rubbing against itself. She pulled away, feeling for Huracan's next move.

35

The Roots

Papa Bois sank beneath the mountain, feeling the scrape of every stone, every moist clump of dirt, and the twisting, tangled roots of every plant brush past his skin. He buried himself deep and then felt for all the roots of all the plants through the island.

They all reached for him, sending tendrils twining against one another, wrapping themselves like hair, like fingers, entangled.

They held together until Papa Bois was more root than creature, until all that seemed to be left of him were the eyes that pierced through the ground, seeing past the rocks and dirt and plants, through to the water that thrashed around the island.

36

Fighting the Sea

The current was riotous and unwieldy. Mama D'Leau turned within it like a piece of rotten wood. The mermaids had arrived only to be tossed about in the undertow created by Huracan's winds.

Mama D'Leau refused to be pinned down again. She whipped her tail, cracking it against the current, trying to bend it to her will, but she flailed in the water and had to grab on to the edge of a piece of broken coral to steady herself. The coral cut into her hand but she didn't let go. As blood darkened the water, Mama

D'Leau sensed the smallest of the mermaids trying to reach her.

No, she said. *Others will need your help.*

The mermaids obeyed and moved away as Mama D'Leau fought the sea.

37

A Crack on the Mountain

Dru returned to the large room and listened to the storm rage, cringing with the others each time lightning pierced the sky and thunder rolled. The boys were curled into Hugo's arms, and Dru's siblings were tucked into each other like pieces of a puzzle. They were safe, and she was glad for that, but some were still in danger. Both Pierre and Mrs. Chow strained to see through a window, looking out with fear in their eyes. Corinne and Marlene were gone. Dru could guess where they were, but the wind and rain, lightning strikes, and thunder made it impossible for anyone to go search for them. Aunty Lu stood near the door, trying to soothe the parents, but barring them from opening it to leave.

Dru hoped her friend would be okay, but fear tracked down her spine.

The rumbling got louder and closer.

Dru and the boys tore away from their parents to peek through a sliver in the wall boards. In the silver light of a bolt, they saw a boulder rolling down the hill, cracking more of the mountain as it came, heading straight toward them.

< 221 >

38

Severine's Return

There was no comfortable place in the mountain for the twiggy Severine to rest. All night long, explosions, cracking, and dampness shook her from every cranny.

She folded and unfolded her thin body and scrambled from one tiny crag to the next, trying to find solace. Something drew her upward, where electricity ran through the seams of the rocks. Its power excited her. All night she moved up and up, pulled almost by force to the top of the mountain in time to see two girls stand on the peak, looking up at the sky. The clouds gathered themselves over their heads and shot silver fire like a long, slender arrow to the smaller of the two girls, sending her rolling to the edge.

Severine had lurched to help, but the bigger of the two girls had shed her skin and reached forward, grabbing the little one in a fiery hand. She had steadied her companion and promptly disappeared into the sky, leaving the small child behind.

Severine scuttled forward. Marlene shrieked at the bundle of sticks and bones that was coming toward her, but Severine did not pause. She gathered the squirming girl against her sharp body and looked down into the child's face. Marlene stopped struggling, but her muscles were tight, as if she was waiting for her moment to spring away. Severine waited a moment, too, until the child's pulse calmed. There was something familiar about the warmth and softness of that body.

She remembered the word *sister*, and something at her core began to beat. Then she remembered the word *heart*. She rocked the little girl and smoothed her hair with her fingers. Marlene relaxed a little.

"That girl called me Severine," she said. "But that is not my real name."

Marlene blinked.

"Oh, you want to know what it is?" Severine asked. She reached back, thinking until she found it, and she leaned close to Marlene's ear and whispered.

The rain beat down harder, and the air moved in huge,

booming whooshes above, so Severine began to move down the mountain toward safety.

The girl reached for something on the ground and Severine turned to look. She was reaching for a large yellow calabash gourd. In it was a pile of skin.

Severine scooped it up and took it with them.

39

Hold Tight

The earth quaked and rocks cracked at their core, ripping down into the ground and tearing the entire island apart.

Papa Bois held on as tightly as he could, but some of the roots slipped from his fingers and snapped away from his body.

He extended his arms to their full length, willing the plants to come closer, to knit the tears in the ground and hold them tight, but he could feel the island slipping away. Pain tore through his muscles and he whimpered as he tried to hold on, as pieces of the land disappeared into the sea.

He almost wanted to go with them.

< 225 >

40

Fire in the Water

The shock of the lightning blast ripped through Mama D'Leau's body. It slashed from the top of her head to the tip of her tail. She felt gutted and was sure she was bleeding as she drifted to the bottom like a sunken vessel.

The water churned over her and the mermaids returned, surrounding her and lifting her from the sea-floor. They ferried her away. She could just barely feel their hands, and the delicate brush of their fins against her body, and their soft singing willing her to gather strength again.

As soon as the pain subsided, Mama D'Leau pushed the mermaids away and returned to the middle of the sea, where the strongest force of the wind was whipping the water into a frenzy. She sent every creature scampering out of the way, moving the currents to take them to safety even more quickly as she careened into the center of the storm. Electricity in the water burned her skin, but what was a little fire in the water, eh? She had seen worse. Hadn't she? Well. If not, it would make a good story in the end. And all stories came to an end eventually.

Mama D'Leau found the very center of the storm, where the water whirled and directed its full force toward her body. Every floating piece of dreck, every sharp stone, every broken bit of coral hurtled itself at Mama D'Leau, powered by the water and the brunt of Huracan's rage. As the debris battered her body, Mama D'Leau whipped her tail under her, back and forth, back and forth, gathering strength, but moving steadily as a jump rope, waiting for the right moment to strike.

41

A Mermaid Found a Swimming Lad

People splashed into the water, falling as all the nearby islands shook and crumbled away. With Mama D'Leau tackling the currents, Noyi and the other two mermaids darted through the sea, gathering people up, pushing them onto floating trees, protruding rocks, and anything else they could find. They rushed to round up as many of the fallen as they could.

We will never get them all, Sisi worried.

We will do what we can, said Addie.

Why do we even bother? Noyi snapped. *If they cannot survive in the water, what good are they at all?*

Nevertheless all three of them exhausted themselves, pushing people back to shore, depositing them into boats that had come unmoored in the storm, and anchoring those as best they could.

Noyi moved a little more slowly than the others, just enough that they would notice, but not so much that they would chastise her about it.

One large boat rocked far from land, filled with screaming people whose voices were whisked away by the wind. The boat tossed in the waves, bashed from all sides until a small boy was thrown out. Sisi caught him, but someone from the boat dove after him. The diver was tall and lithe and swam through the churning sea better than anyone they had saved that night, but even he couldn't swim through a hurricane.

Noyi shook her head, but reached for him anyway. When her hand touched his, he found her eyes, and Noyi felt the warmth of his body extend to her own.

Another body splashed into the water, and another. The boat had overturned. The diver pulled his hand from Noyi's, looked at one sinking frame, and pointed at another. Noyi understood. The boy went right and she went left, gathering up those who had fallen in and pushing them to the surface.

< 229 >

They both breached water and the boy took a gulp of breath.

Lightning flashed above them, and they saw the outline of another body sinking beneath. Without a word, the two dove, splashing down to reach the tiny form of a toddler whose dress billowed out behind her as she sank.

Amazingly, the boy got there first and handed the child to Noyi, who rushed her to air and into the arms of her waiting mother, who was being ferried by Addie to the nearest shore.

Noyi turned, expecting the boy to surface behind her, but he did not.

She looked into the water and smiled when she saw him, his arms reaching out to her. Her heart caught and she paused, waiting for him to arrive, but his face changed, from calm to anguish in an instant, and he opened his mouth.

He gasped bubbles, pulling one hand to his throat.

Noyi raced to him and caught his limp hand to drag him to the surface. She turned his face up toward air and patted his back. She pulled him close to her body, hoping to feel his warmth again, but it was slowly draining away.

It was too late for him.

42

Ready

The air around Corinne tightened and loosened, tightened and loosened, in the rhythm of a pacing animal. Corinne understood this. She knew trapped creatures, ones that were frustrated, ones that were preparing to attack.

Her heart beat wildly, but she willed herself to take a deep breath and another until her heart slowed and thudded in a steady rhythm. Now was not the time for panic. She needed to be able to think, to move. The air squeezed and released again.

She was ready.

43

The Lagahoo

The boulder splintered as it hit the ground, but it still tumbled toward the center of the village, groaning as it came, mashing down everything in its path.

People spilled out of the doors, onto the slick, muddy ground. There was a lot of slipping and grasping of hands and pulling as the air was filled with screams and gasps of panic and the squelching of mud underfoot.

Mr. and Mrs. Rootsingh gathered up their children and ran, but Mrs. Rootsingh tripped on the end of her sari. Dru ran back and tried to pull her mama to her feet.

The rock tumbled on, nearly as tall as a house, and it was not slowing down. The tall, lanky man from the caves saw it rolling toward them. He sighed. He had done everything he could to hide in the crowd, but now he was needed. And it would take all of his strength to help, even the strands of energy he used to make himself look human. He looked at Dru and her mama.

Dru slipped and fell on her back. Mrs. Rootsingh spotted the boulder and tried to shove Dru out of the way.

The man turned, slipping in the wet grass, and as he did, his body changed. Already tall, he lengthened even more. His shoulders widened, and the hair all over his body thickened. He loped toward Mrs. Rootsingh and Dru as his nose and mouth grew into a wolf's snout from which rows of sharp, yellow teeth protruded. Now fully his lagahoo self, he scooped the two of them up and kept going. He skidded off to the side as the rock rumbled past, squeezing the earth where they had just been a moment before.

The lagahoo felt the woman and girl struggling against him, so he let them go and backed away. Dru got to her feet and held her mama's arm.

His sharp fur left pinpricks all over their skin.

"That thing nearly killed you!" Victor called. "Do you see?"

"It . . . he saved us," Dru said.

The rock hurtled to one side of the plateau, went up the lip of the wall, and careened back their way.

The boulder smashed through a small house and

crushed the top of a well and the side of the communal cooking area, but it still kept coming. It was slower than before, but no less dangerous.

The lagahoo went back, looking for stragglers.

"Get out of here!" Victor screamed. "We don't need your help." He tried to pick up something from the ground, but slipped and fell flat on his face.

The lagahoo looked at him briefly, but continued on.

Victor twisted in the mud and tried to get to his knees, but he slipped again and fell on his back. Everything he did to get up landed him flat in the mud.

The rock bowled toward him.

The lagahoo looked back and sighed. Then it jogged to Victor.

Victor just got his feet under him and looked back to see the rock coming at him from one side and the lagahoo from the other. The only way to get away from both was toward the cliff.

He ran.

As the rock closed in, Victor skidded to the edge and tried to come to a stop, but couldn't. His arms flailed over his head as he teetered on the same ledge that Mama D'Leau had leapt from.

44

Take the Hit

The air around Corinne prickled with heat. Pops of electricity pinched and bored into her body. She closed her eyes, feeling Huracan gather his energy. Beneath him was the energy of all the people in the islands. Their fear shivered up to the clouds. Corinne sensed the strain of Papa Bois's muscles as he held on to the very dust to keep the island together and the whip of Mama D'Leau's tail as she tried to calm the water.

They were both badly hurt and couldn't take much more.

They had done their part, but Corinne had not been

able to stop Huracan. She hadn't landed a blow, or tired him out. Maybe she could beg.

"I have had enough," Huracan said in a voice that rolled deeply around Corinne.

"If you destroy everyone, who will be left to remember you?" Corinne asked.

The air thinned and strengthened again. "There is always someone left," the god rumbled. The pressure thickened around Corinne. "But it will not be you."

Corinne felt heavy. There was no way to stop a god.

The blow was coming. She felt it gathering power.

She opened her eyes. Whatever happened next, she was going to watch it happen straight on.

45

Fire in the Sky

The child was irritating. Like a stone in your side that took an age to wear away or a cacophony of souls all talking at once.

Huracan was tired. He had been tired. This was one in a long succession of waves of fatigue that overcame him any time he roused from his sleep. Once, there had been no voices at all, and when they came, he would awaken, roar in the skies, hurtle the winds, stir up the seas, and after, it would be quiet again.

He missed the quiet.

The child was nothing like he had seen before. She was quick. She had figured out how to move around him, to anticipate where he would be, and to duck from his grasp. Worst of all, she was persistent.

The god moved around the child in a huffing swirl of cloud. She adjusted her position as he moved. Even when he didn't manifest into a solid shape, somehow she knew where he was.

Clever.

Annoying.

Electricity crackled around Huracan like a spiked cloak. He knew it hurt her to occupy the same air as him. He was thrilled that it did, and yet she would not simply return to earth. She was relentless. And she had talked back. Never had anyone shouted him down.

He gathered his strength, assembling the sparking, crackling energy of the air into a single sharp weapon.

Huracan laughed to himself as he felt Corinne stiffen and her heart race. This was the end. Of her. Of all of them.

But then she opened her eyes and looked straight through him, and he shivered with dread.

No one made him feel like that!

The air sparked and popped around them.

Huracan focused his energy at the center of Corinne's chest. At first, he had felt sorry for her, but now? He would welcome her end. There was symmetry to it. She would die the same way that her mother had.

Huracan felt a twinge around him, as if something in the air had changed, but it wasn't the time to be distracted.

He turned the full force of his energy to the girl, roaring and screaming as the lightning bolt ripped through the air to Corinne's heart.

It crashed into her with a satisfying crunch, and the sky exploded in flashes of white and red. The stone at her throat exploded into shards. Huracan felt satisfied, but only for a moment until the force of the hit blew back to him, blasting him apart.

Wisps of him scattered in every direction at once.

Beneath, the earth trembled and water spouted, reaching straight to the child, searing the air.

Every fragment of the god focused on Corinne. She was a shimmering creature of fire and lightning, flesh and fur and scales, dripping with seawater.

It was only then that the god understood.

He felt the satyr underground harnessing the strength of the land, and the siren gathering the energy of the water. The girl had called for help. She was not alone.

He wanted to roar again, to strike one more time, but it was too late for that. Huracan had used up everything he had. He was nothing now, only threads of vapor floating in the darkness.

He saw her eyes searching for him in the sky as she began to fall.

It was the end.

For now.

46

The Last Save

Dru strained her eyes to watch as the boulder tipped
over the cliff, taking some of the retaining wall with
it, but rolling past Victor.

The lagahoo who had saved Dru and her mother
reached for Victor. Dru saw the sharp fur of the creature's
back as it hunched over the cliff. It groaned, then pulled
hard, and Victor came tossing back up and over, splat, into
the mud. He blinked up at the lagahoo but said nothing.
The creature growled at him, baring its saliva-covered
teeth.

Above the village, the sky exploded in brilliant color.
A shockwave flattened the people, pushing them into the

earth, and knocked over some of the buildings already teetering on their foundations.

The force made Dru's ears pop. Everything went silent. People peeled themselves off the ground. The rain changed to a light mist and then petered out entirely. The clouds opened up and revealed the first pinpricks of stars in the sky.

Slowly, the expressions in the crowd changed to relief, and then wide smiles.

Bouki and Malik pulled Dru to her feet. Hugo and Aunty Lu walked toward them side by side. The baker said something and Aunty Lu laughed.

Dru heard ringing in her ears and then a loud rush, like the roar of the sea. The sound of mud squelching underfoot came after, and of people talking all at once. Up ahead, Pierre and Mrs. Chow ran, full speed, toward the peak.

Malik pointed into the sky.

"Look!" Bouki said. He pointed in the same direction as his brother.

Something was falling. Fast.

47

Mon Coeur

The sky turned a brighter shade of blue.

The sea, still midnight-dark, pushed debris onto shore. Broken branches, leaves, and small pieces of stone and coral lined the fringes of water in a long, rippling scroll that matched the edge of the waves.

Among the dreck lay a beautiful woman with dark skin that glowed like copper in the predawn light. Her tightly braided hair spread around her face. She wore a pale blue blouse and a brighter blue skirt in a pattern that shimmered like stars. A man with long braided hair emerged from a screen of leaves near the shore. He fell

< 242 >

to his knees near the woman and gently brushed a braid from her face.

"Cherie," he said.

The woman stirred and lifted her head toward him. She traced the outline of a few wrinkles around his eyes and a scar that wrapped like a vine over his arm. "*Mon coeur!*"

"So, we have decided then," he said. "We cannot go back."

"Everything is right here," she said. "What is there to miss?"

The man pulled her to standing and the two walked into the trees.

48

Things You Do for Family

Pierre observed the couple from the space at the top of the hill where his home with Corinne had been. He wasn't watching for Papa Bois and Mama D'Leau, of course, or for their human selves. He was watching for Corinne like he always did, whether he was on land or on the sea.

After the hurricane ended, he and Mrs. Chow had scrambled toward the top of the mountain. They came to a halt in front of the twiggy creature holding Marlene. Mrs. Chow approached it carefully, holding out her arms, and the creature had given up the child easily.

"Severine?" Pierre said.

Severine rubbed her branches together, squeaking in response.

Mrs. Chow removed the wrap she had tied around her waist and placed it over Severine's body.

"Where is Corinne?" Pierre asked.

A thin twig pointed up to the sky and then traced down to the sea.

Pierre collapsed against a boulder.

"Don't forget, she will need her skin," Marlene said quietly. She pointed at the calabash gourd in Severine's long, hard fingers.

Severine straightened up, rearranging herself into something nearly like a woman. "I will get her," she said. She dashed off down the side of the mountain, head over twiggy foot, bouncing over the rocks with the calabash safely nestled among her limbs.

Pierre had no choice but to climb down the mountain. As he made his way back to the house, he thought about what he had overheard Papa Bois and Mama D'Leau talking about—being their true selves. If that was what Corinne needed, for them all to do what they were best at, Pierre had failed. He was best at taking care of Corinne, but it felt like a long time since he had been able to do that well. His body was weary and his heart was heavy in his chest.

It was still dark when he arrived and found their home flattened, with just the foundation and stairs left standing.

He sat at the top of the hill and scanned the sky and the sea. He didn't feel the cool breeze, or the hard ground.

In the first rays of morning light, he picked out the pieces of their lives that had survived the hurricane. There was a cup and the knives they used to slice the fish, the lone dress Corinne ever wore, and the left sandal of a leather pair that had gotten too small for her growing feet.

Pierre piled them on one of the stone foundation pillars and sat against it, watching the sea and sky. In one hand he held a warm orange from Corinne's tree. He had found it half-buried in the dirt in the middle of the wreckage of the house. He turned it over and over. Its scent was strong and sharp and sweet. *Like Corinne*, he thought.

Pierre waited hour after hour until he was nearly blinded by the sunlight reflecting off the waves. Slowly people from the fishing village filtered back to their homes and began the long, aching work of pulling out what little there was to save.

Below on the beach, Laurent and his little brothers and sisters helped Mrs. Duval. Laurent was minding the younger ones as they searched for things they had loved among all the mess.

Pierre used one of the knives to peel the orange. He ate it, and he waited.

When the sun was high in the sky, Marlene arrived at the top of the hill.

"Mr. La Mer?" she said.

"Yes, Marlene?"

"Miss will bring her back," she said. "I told her what to do with Corinne's skin."

Pierre held back tears. "Thank you, Marlene."

Marlene held her hand out to Pierre. "Come." Marlene led him around the debris and toward the beach. They went down the hill to the lacy fringe of waves that continued to push items onto shore. A comb. A necklace of beads. A hair ribbon.

Two dark spots appeared on the horizon, and then another and another. They got larger as Pierre and Marlene watched.

"Boats!" Marlene declared.

The people on the beach looked up from their salvage work and watched the boats come in. When the vessels came close, their occupants began to tumble out. They had nothing in their hands, little on their backs, and desperation in their eyes.

"We have lost everything," a man said as he set foot on shore.

Pierre grabbed the rope the man tossed to him, and together they pulled the boat from the water.

"Our island is flat," the man continued. "There is not even a single leaf on a tree."

Nearly everyone from the fishing village moved into the water to gather up the people from the boats and help them onto dry land.

"Where are these people from?" Victor snarled. "We lost everything, too. They should go back home."

"You should shut up," Laurent said sharply as he took a wailing baby while his own mother helped the baby's shivering mother out of the boat.

People came out of their homes with blankets, sheets, curtains—anything dry enough to wrap around the shivering refugees.

"Fools!" Victor snapped. "What will you sleep under?"

Abner handed a piece of board to Victor. It was green, the color of his fishing boat. "That is yours, mister," he said. "I can help you fix it."

Victor glared. "You?"

"We help each other, and I am good with a hammer."

"No, he is not," Mrs. Duval said, cocking an eyebrow. But a smile pulled at her mouth. "But he is right. We do help one another, Victor. Here." She handed him a small, wriggling boy. "Make yourself useful."

Victor deposited the boy in the sand gently. "Stay," he said a little gruffly. "It's safe here." Then he returned to the boat and steadied it as more people poured out.

All day, boats arrived and people poured from them, sandy, starved, thirsty, and distraught.

Night came again, and there was no Corinne. Pierre and Marlene waited, watching the sun sink, until Mrs. Chow took Marlene's hand and pulled her home. Marlene gave Pierre a hard look, as if she was pinning him to the shore to wait.

It was the first thing that made Pierre smile that day.

When the moon was high, Hugo, Bouki, and Malik came to persuade Pierre to join them in the bakery.

"We've got two families from the boats," Hugo explained. "But there's plenty more room for you, Pierre." He glanced up at the house on the hill. "You need somewhere to stay."

Pierre shook his head, but he was convinced to take a small meal of two cheese loaves. Only when he unwrapped the brown paper, it was one and a half loaves.

"Sorry," Bouki said, wiping a crumb from the side of his mouth.

Malik kicked him in the ankle.

It was the second thing that made Pierre smile that day.

Something rocked on the surface of the water as Pierre bit into what remained of his meal. All four of them walked cautiously toward the shape. It was a tangle of branches, cupped like a nest, with someone curled inside it, lying on a brightly colored scarf.

"Corinne," Pierre said softly.

A creature peeked out that was Corinne and not Corinne. It had her soft brown eyes and the long hair that Pierre carefully plaited every night, but where Corinne's bright smile should have been, drool dripped from sharp teeth in a red, angry mouth. Her body was covered in scales, fish-bright on one side and snake-dull on the other. One of her hands was dark as ash with blue flame playing around the fingers. The other was hairy at the knuckles with claws at the end of her fingers. One leg ended in a floppy fish tail with a bright orange fin, while the other was a girl's leg with a goat's hoof where the foot should be.

"What is that?" Bouki said.

Malik squinted at the nest. "Corinne."

Hugo gasped but Pierre was still. He reached out carefully to pull the nest to shore. Hugo, Bouki, and Malik each took one part of the nest and dragged it to the sand.

The thing that was Corinne and not Corinne sniffed at Pierre and growled.

Pierre reached his hand to her slowly.

Malik put his hand in, too, and smiled.

Then Hugo.

Bouki cocked his head at her and narrowed his eyes.

Corinne finally moved her flame hand toward her papa's. As she did the fire went out, so when they touched, her hand was the same brown it had always been.

Pierre offered his other hand.

Corinne and not Corinne grabbed it and Pierre pulled gently. Her claws scratched at him, but he didn't flinch. Her eyes softened. Then her mouth plumped from an angry red line to soft pink lips. Corinne got to her knees. The fish scales on her right fell away like sugar crystals off a tamarind ball. The snake scales on her left smoothed out to deep brown. Her claws retracted and the coarse brown hair on her arms blew away in a soft breeze.

Pierre reached in, taking Corinne out. She lifted her legs up and over the side of the nest. As she touched water, the fish tail dissolved and her right foot softened and unfurled. On the left, her hoof changed to wriggling toes. By the time she splashed down in the water, there were only a few orange scales left clinging to her clothes. Pierre gathered her up in his arms.

"Papa," Corinne said.

"Welcome home," Pierre said.

Corinne pointed to the water where the tangle of branches was rearranging itself until it was Severine again. Severine tied the scarf around herself and stepped out of the water, holding the calabash gourd stiffly in front of her as if she might need to use it for protection.

"Thank you," Pierre said to the jumbie.

Severine glanced sheepishly at him and whispered, "I told you I would find her."

49

Wire Bend

Corinne sat between Mrs. Duval's knees on the front steps of the porch. She held a measuring cup filled with orange beads, which Mrs. Duval was threading on the ends of Corinne's braids. Nearby, Laurent had a can of pink paint that he slathered on the fresh wood walls in big brushstrokes.

"There," Mrs. Duval said. "Perfect."

Corinne shook her head and the beads clicked in rhythm.

"You'd better go, or you will miss everything," Mrs. Duval added.

Corinne bowed her thanks and slapped Laurent on

the arm. "You will meet me there?" she asked before running off.

He nodded and waved the paintbrush, dripping pink on the grass and a red-and-yellow croton plant.

Corinne topped the hill and ran full out, past the mahogany forest that was springing up with young trees.

Two tall men, larger than seemed possible (and hairier, too), came out of the woods shouldering a pair of logs. They walked to an empty lot near the old dry well and heaved the logs onto a pile. Another man, smaller than the first two, was cutting the logs into planks with an axe. A sawhorse stood surrounded by curled wood chips near where they had been planing each plank smooth. The wood smelled sweetly of oranges and mahogany. As Corinne walked by, the largest of the men smiled, showing sharp teeth. The skin around his yellowish-brown eyes crinkled. Corinne waved hello. It made her smile to see the lagahoo trying out their human forms, enough that they almost looked like family to the man who was helping them build.

Corinne skipped toward the marketplace, her newly sewn dress swinging around her. It was a small green thing with a pattern of darker green leaves, and it fluttered around her knees. She had a freshly cobbled pair of leather sandals on her feet that squeaked a little when she moved. It felt unusual not to be wearing her work clothes, but today wasn't a workday. Not for her.

Corinne ducked under a pair of women carrying a

long bolt of cloth in their arms. She greeted them and they smiled back, but their faces weren't familiar. Past the full well and down the path that led to the baker's shop, Corinne dodged people walking with baskets of produce on their heads or tin buckets filled with screws and nails.

All around her, the air smelled of wood and grass and cotton and sweat.

Corinne knocked on the bakery door. It was not a workday for the baker either. His work had been done the day before, though she was sure there would be a few last-minute touches.

Bouki swung open the top of the Dutch door. "A dress!" he said, grinning. "Is that what took you so long?" He unlatched the rest of the door and he and Malik spilled out. "Hugo left early, and we're missing all the food."

Corinne arched an eyebrow at the boys' crisp embroidered shirts and short pants with sharply ironed seams.

"This was Hugo's idea," Bouki said. "I told him we were fine in our regular clothes."

"Not for a wedding," Corinne said.

They took off at a fast pace. Near the marketplace, Marlene caught up with them. She was in a pink dress with blue flowers. Matching pink ribbons were tied tightly in her pigtails. When Malik hung back for her, she put her hand in his.

"I like your shorts," she said.

"I like your ribbons," Malik replied.

They swung hands and took off skipping ahead.

"Are you going to explain what happened to Huracan?" Bouki asked Corinne.

She took a deep breath. "I was scared," she admitted. "He was strong. Stronger than Severine. Stronger than Papa Bois and Mama D'Leau. I didn't know what I could do to stop him, so I decided that I wouldn't. He wanted to strike me with his lightning. He was going to do it no matter what. I could feel everyone straining below in the water and under the land, doing their part, and somehow I knew that my part was to take the hit." She paused.

"Well?" Bouki shouted.

"He threw a bolt of lightning at me, and I opened my eyes to see what would happen. He had been so angry all along, but right then his face softened. I think he was surprised and maybe a little bit glad that he hadn't killed me. When the lightning hit me, it didn't hurt. It was like a surge of energy. Fire burst out in every direction, burning away the clouds until only his eyes were left watching me fall. Then they faded, too.

"I don't remember falling into the water, or Severine getting me out. The next thing I knew was being on shore with my papa."

"Do you think Huracan is gone for good?" Bouki asked.

Corinne looked around at all the new faces in town. Some from nearby islands, others from deep in the mahogany forest. "I don't think so."

Corinne looked past the cracked stone at the market-place entryway to a bare spot in the middle of the square. The lone tree where the white witch once sold her wares had fallen in the storms. A family had taken its wood to repair their house.

People were bustling about, buying and selling. A tall, dark woman with impossibly long eyelashes and an enchanting smile walked with a bit of a hitch across the market. Severine. She carried a large calabash gourd in the crook of her left arm and stopped occasionally to show people what was inside.

"How much do you think she remembers?" Bouki asked Corinne.

"Not much right now," Corinne said. "But she remembers that we are family."

"What is going to happen when she remembers everything?" he asked as Severine pulled out a long necklace for a customer and pocketed a few coins.

"Then she will be able to tell me about my mother."

Severine spotted them and waved. "Morning," she said brightly.

"Hello Miss!" Marlene sang.

"Morning, Tante Severine," Corinne said.

"Miss Severine," Bouki said.

"I have something for you, Corinne." Severine reached into the gourd and pulled out a necklace of silk cloth into which three stones had been sewn. "I know you lost your own, so I tried to find something that might make up for it." She pointed to the first stone. "I found this one in the sea," she said, indicating one that gleamed like rain on a spider's web. "And this one, I found in the heart of the mountain." She showed one that was black on the outside with a hint of purple at a cracked edge. "And this one fell right out of the sky." It was rough and white and cool to the touch.

Severine tied the necklace on Corinne's neck. It fell beneath her collarbone, just over her heart. Each stone pressed against her skin like the light touch of a hand.

"Thank you," she said.

"I know it is not the same," Severine said.

Corinne squeezed her aunt's bony fingers. "It's good," she said.

"We are *really* missing all the food," Bouki complained. "Dahl, rice, curry goat . . ." He rolled his eyes and staggered off holding his stomach for added drama.

• • •

Loud laughter, singing, and the rhythm of tassa drums greeted the four children near the end of the long, dusty road at the far side of Dru's village. They ran to catch up. It seemed as if everyone from the nearby villages was sitting under the white tent at long tables, eating off large, glossy banana leaves. In one corner, a group of three men in white, two of them with drums hanging from straps around their necks and the third with a pair of small cymbals, played music. They chucked their feet and shook their shoulders to the fast beat, while a few people danced.

Bouki abandoned Corinne for an empty spot at the end of one of the tables. Arjun, Dru's brother, plopped a whole pot spoon of curried chickpeas on the leaf, followed by Karma with a spoonful of rice. Vidia splashed watermelon juice into Bouki's cup. Bouki barely mumbled thanks before he dug in with his fingers. A moment later, Dru herself, in a pale blue sari with a thin gold bangle on one arm, put a small spoonful of anchar on his leaf.

Bouki dug into the anchar, and then reached for the watermelon juice when his eyes began to water.

"I should have warned you, it's very spicy," Dru said.

Bouki panted. "It's perfect!"

Corinne and Dru giggled. Dru moved on, following her siblings up and down the tables. They put more food on banana leaves in front of each guest, then fell back to the temporary kitchen behind the tent to refill their serving bowls.

Corinne ate a little and went to find where Hugo had set up the cake.

It was off to the side of the kitchen in a cooler spot under the tent, in the shade of a large cashew tree that had managed to survive the storms. Hugo pressed little gold sugar balls into each of the delicate red flowers that covered the three tiers of the yellow-frosted cake. The entire thing gleamed.

"Do you need help?" Corinne asked.

"No, no," Hugo said.

"Is it finished?" Fatima peeked from behind a flap in the tent in a red sari embroidered in gold. Her hands were elaborately decorated with henna, and gold bangles on both arms clinked as she tried to get a good look. A delicate gold chain went from her ear to her nose ring, and bright red and orange flowers formed a crown on her head. Her eyes were ringed in black kohl, and her lips were as red as the flowers on the cake.

"Yes, it's ready," Hugo said. He stepped back to admire his own work.

"Can I take a little taste?" Fatima asked.

"Where are you, Fatima!" Mrs. Rootsingh called sharply. "You are not supposed to be out here."

Fatima ducked back behind the canopy, and Corinne watched as her henna-covered feet danced off, each step causing her anklets to jingle.

"She's in trouble," Marlene said. She got up on a chair to take a better look at the cake. Hugo put her back on the ground, away from the cake, and handed her the small bowl of gold sugar balls. Marlene popped a couple of them in her mouth and passed the bowl to Corinne, who popped in a couple, too. They were hard at first, but melted on her tongue after she rolled them around a bit.

Malik bounded up and grabbed a handful of sugar balls. Bouki came and stood near Corinne.

The Rootsinghs had told everyone about the wedding, and all who could come brought food. One of the families new to the island hung at the edge of the festivities, looking for a place to sit. Pierre came in behind them and ushered them to a spot at a nearby table. Dru and her siblings immediately filed over to put fresh banana leaves in front of them and serve the food.

One of the tall builders Corinne had seen on the road earlier ducked under the tent and looked around. He crouched a bit, as if he was trying to hide his enormous frame. Dru took his hand and brought him to another table at the far end of the tent. As he sat on the bench, it tipped toward him, and several people slid into his side. The man looked nervous until everyone roared with laughter. He joined in, with a little bit of a howl.

People from other islands, people who had come from the depths of the forest, and people who had lived on this island their entire lives were all sitting together, eating and shaking their bodies to the rhythm of the tassa. If Corinne squinted her eyes, she couldn't tell who came from where. Here, under the canopy for Fatima's wedding, they all belonged together.

"Oh, hello hello!" called a booming voice from the other side of the canopy. A large shadow fell on the side of the tent as the woman it belonged to tried to find the opening. Pierre got up to help her. He held the canopy open, and Aunty Lu came in, wearing a dress in a rainbow of colors and a matching head tie knotted into a huge bow in her hair. Several others from the mountain village trailed behind her. "What's this?" she exclaimed as she looked around at the party. "And where is the bride?"

"This is for everyone to eat," Dru explained. "The bride isn't supposed to be out yet."

Fatima ducked behind one of the cloths at the back.

"Oh, you eat first?" Aunty Lu asked. "That's delightful!"

Dru showed them to a bench near the cake.

Hugo smiled nervously and wrung his hands. "I suppose I should be polite and say hello," he whispered to no one in particular. "She is their aunt after all. I am only . . ."

"Our papa," Bouki said.

Hugo's smile brightened and his entire body seemed to soften under his starched white smock. "Yes," he said. "Let us say hello."

Hugo and Bouki stepped across to Aunty Lu and her party as Malik skipped over and threw his hands around his aunt's neck.

"When will we see you again?" she asked.

"Soon," Hugo said. "We will make a trip up the mountain next week."

"Make it a long trip, eh," Aunty Lu said. "We will want you for a few days."

"Hello Corinne!" Allan beamed. His hair had been

washed and slicked back with coconut oil, and from the shine on his face and skin, the whole of him might have been oiled down, too.

"Hi, Allan."

"Hey there, little douen," Bouki said.

Allan quickly looked down at his feet. "I am not a douen," he said.

"Not today," Bouki teased.

"Excuse me, what is that? A dweh . . . a . . ." the woman from the new family asked. "We keep hearing stories about things that live in the forests, things that will . . . well . . . eat you."

Corinne looked at her friends. "You mean the douens," Corinne said. "That's nothing. It's only a jumbie story, things to frighten children at bedtime." She made tickly claw-hands at the little girl sitting between the woman and man. The child giggled.

"So they are not real? There are no creatures like that living in the woods?" the man asked.

The tall, hairy man looked over at them stiffly.

Dru put some more food in front of the family. "There's nothing to worry about here," she said.

The parents looked relieved.

The tall, hairy man tucked back into his curried goat.

Laurent appeared at the canopy doorway holding a bottle of red plums. "You forgot to bring these, Marlene," he said. "Mrs. Chow told me to give them to you." But instead of handing them over, he unscrewed the top, pulled out a plum, and popped it in his mouth.

"Hey!" Marlene said.

Laurent resealed the jar and handed it to Marlene. "I love weddings," he said.

Bouki patted his stomach. "What's not to love?"

The little girl sitting with her parents reached out and yanked the hem of Corinne's dress. "So will you tell me a jumbie story?"

Corinne leaned down. "Sure," she said. "But they are very scary."

"I like scary stories," the girl said.

Corinne cleared her throat. "Once there was a child who thought she could do everything on her own," she began. "But she couldn't. So a jumbie ate her."

The child's eyes went wide, and everyone started laughing. Malik tapped Corinne on the shoulder and passed her a piece of wire.

"Oh," Corinne said. "There's something else you should know."

"What's that?" the little girl asked.

Corinne twisted the wire around the girl's finger. "It's something we say when we're finished telling a story," she said.

"What do you say?" her mother asked.

In a chorus of giggles, Corinne and her friends said all together: "Wire bend, story end."

Acknowledgments

There wasn't supposed to be a third jumbies book. There wasn't even supposed to be a second one. But at the beginning of what would become this series, I envisioned three stories, one on land, one in the sea, and one in the sky. I knew what I'd do for the first two. How I would manage a sky story, though, I had no idea. So, with the second book I decided to put everything in, leaving no room for a third. Then Elise Howard called me in Trinidad in August 2017 and suggested we make it a trilogy. My mind was blank. That evening I had dinner with my mom, my two children, and my aunt and uncle in Siparia, the village where I spent the first eight years of my life. Together they concocted the idea of Jumbies in Space. This isn't that. But it got me started.

Many thanks to my family, despite their terrible, though hilarious, suggestions, especially my mother, Gloria; my children, Alyssa and Adam; and Waynie and Wendy (my uncle and aunt), for getting me out of a slump. As always, I couldn't do any of this without my husband, Darryl, and his constant, unwavering support. I'm also fortunate to have a dad who's only too happy to fact-check. I'm eternally grateful to my editors: Elise Howard, for pushing me in the best of ways, and Sarah Alpert, for keeping me in line and on track. I'm lucky to have the support of Marie Lamba and the entire Jennifer De Chiara Literary team, and thanks especially to my assistant, Esperanza Pacheco, for making so many things easier. For daily moral support, occasional reading, general ego boosting, good cheer, and camaraderie I have a coterie of ladies to thank: Kelly Barnhill, Martha Brockenbrough, Kate Messner, Olugbemisola Rhuday-Perkovich, Laura Ruby, Laurel Snyder, Linda Urban, and Anne Ursu. What would I do without you?